Needles and Skins

SAM STILTON

Spicy Plurals Media Ltd

First published 2013 by Spicy Plurals Media Ltd
38 Winton Crescent, Blantyre, G72 0QN

Cover design by Spicy Plurals Media Ltd
Cover artwork by Nancy Holt

ISBN 978-0-9927287-0-0

spicy-plurals-media.co.uk

This book is dedicated in the memory of my late brother and sister.

Acknowledgements;

My thanks to Michael Walsh, for his initial encouragement and advice, ongoing mentoring and editing.

To Nancy Holt owner of www.andalucianartists.com for her beautiful cover artwork.

To the staff and owners of Spicy Plurals Media Ltd for their assistance and advice in bringing this book to print, as well as the final editing and initial marketing.

Chapter 1
Reveille

Like she was sitting in a drum the walls seemed to reverberate as she yelled, 'Get fucking up, now!'

'Oh no, not again! I thought to myself. I am so cream crackered. What time is it?' It's still dark so I wouldn't have known what time it was. I was well aware this was a school day but not for the first time found myself wondering how my alcoholic mother remembered. It was instinct maybe. Despite her drink problems you couldn't fault her sergeant-major methods of discipline. 'Right, fuck face. Stick your 'ead out - because you know who I fucking well mean.'

As I joined my three sisters and brother on the couch I too became a fully paid up member of the Wide Awake Club. Young as we were we had the brains to know when to keep quiet. A sidelong glance at mother was asking for the slipper and not necessarily across the arse. She was adept at using the slipper as freely as she used her tongue.

Mother acquired this life skill from her Irish Catholic mother. The lady had carried ten children altogether leaving aside the ones that never reached the cot. Sissy had been a good hard working woman. She was wed to an alcoholic Irish husband, a refugee from the depression years. It was rumoured that he was a bit of a player and as a skirt chaser he would shag a mossy grid. That all changed after he came back from the Great War. In some battle or other he had lost a leg to gangrene. That was the tale told; but who knows? The rumours were always in abundance in this family. Anyway, did anyone really care when everyone had their own bleak lives to cope with?

Sissy was a physically strong and hardened woman who had endured much misery and hardship in her life. A born in the wool matriarch she was in her element only when complaining about anything and everything. The matriarch was adamant that all things had to be just so. Meat had to be bought from a particular butcher. In her eyes, if it didn't come from 'Wilson's' then it simply wasn't meat. She point blank refused to buy bread from a Pakistani-owned store even if it was wrapped. She fervently believed it to be contaminated with curryitus or whatever Asian sounding like disease she could dream up.

Racism or preference for her own kind; a rose by any other name is still a rose. It was just one of a few of her strange beliefs. Sissy had quite a few interesting little rituals to her credit. One was to prick her cigarette because she thought the effects would get stronger. Haggard beyond her years, worn down by life, Sissy constantly scolded and scowled and enforced her commands with the slipper.

The slipper was a commonly used pacifier. In those days no one would think twice about using it for the slightest or even a perceived sin. Any sin so great as to render the slipper inadequate to meet the need; then the belt came off. The leather belt was wrapped around the knuckles and when used was just short of lethal. You knew you really were in deep trouble when the belt came off. You didn't argue. If you protested or squealed you got it behind the knees.

'Right you', she would say, looking like a woman possessed and appearing much more terrifying than the Exorcist movie. She was seen as a crazy person who, to children aged between three and eight, was not to be messed with. The interrogations would be for silly things;

then there would be a bawled out, 'You!' and the finger jabbing at the accused would begin. It was then we all held our breath and hoped we were not 'the chosen one.'

'Why the fuck did you forget to empty the bins?' she sneered as she was pointing to my brother Alfie; her finger poking at his face. It was an oddity for her to round on Alfie because out of all of us he was her clear favourite. However, when fired up favouritism was put to one side. Putting it quite simply, Sissy was off her face and would have absolutely no recollection of the brutal encounter the following morning.

'You are getting kept in and you are not going oot tomorrow. Now get the fuck out of my sight.' To this day she is still the only women I know who called her kids 'pricks' and 'wankers.' Her doing so amused us in its own strange way. Eventually grandmother would fall asleep. That was our opportunity to sneak off as quiet as mice to avoid waking her.

I had been a five year old mite when we moved to a Glasgow tenement. This address was privately rented from my father's brother. The dole paid for this poky claustrophobic first floor two bedroomed flat. The real tenant meanwhile lived in a fancy area in Glasgow. No, there were no flies on him. With seven of us sharing us kids were all a little squashed to say the least. There was no space and as a consequence tempers flared frequently.

My parents then; were in the same poverty trap that so many Glaswegians found themselves in. Getting credit cheques was an essential lifeline to many tenants but they came with huge interest payments. My aunt was our Provident agent. She was the only person known to us who constantly talked about having porridge again for breakfast. This was to place lying emphasis on her being skint when in truth she had three jobs and lived in a big fancy house. My aunt must have earned a fortune in commission from the 'privy' as most of her customers were her family. Catalogues were also a good source of credit; for some the only way to clothe their families. As a family we didn't know anyone who didn't use catalogues; especially at Christmas. Our family was blacklisted by quite a few of the catalogue companies for not keeping up with the weekly payments. Such sins were considered normal to us and there were never any real consequences. A few missed payments, the inevitable threats and blandishments would stream through the letter box. Then afterwards things would go quiet after a while.

Our family often got itself into a lot of debt but thanks to the credit side of things, we were reasonably well dressed; and at Christmases and birthdays could be sure of receiving gifts. One festive season I clearly recall hiding from the electricity and gas men. My father had conjured up a nifty little trick. He had learnt how to stick a darning needle in the meter to stop it running whilst the supply kept coming. Then, when it was time for the meter readers to call we had to have every fire in the house switched on. Over the few days leading up to the meter reader's scheduled call it was quite a comical routine. When they entered to read the meter, the apartment was as hot as a sauna.

The four rings from the cooker would be blazing and the gas fire was on full blast. This was common practice in such communities as ours. We even had relatives in London who loved nothing more than siphoning off the gas. They got away with the ruse for ages. Then one day the husband ventured outside and asked the man working on the gas why he was disconnected. When the workman checked his records he learnt that he hadn't paid a penny towards the gas for twelve years. Surprise! Surprise! He was fined. Seriously, you couldn't make it up. From a very early age it was drummed into us that you do not open the door to anyone.

The problem with Glasgow's tenements back then was that the main entrance door did not have a secure entry system. Anyone could come off the street and just rap the apartment door. Such knocking is unpredictable and can come at the most unexpected times. On one particularly rainy day such a knock would leave an impact.

There was a sharp rapping at our flat door. My sister Deborah was the unfortunate one to innocently open the door. Grief! On opening it she found herself in an eyeball to eyeball confrontation with the man from the Scottish Electricity Board. She had blown it big-style. The golden rule was, before opening the door; you had to ask who was there. She forgot to do so. When the SEB inspector told her he was there to read the meter his eyes settled immediately on the darning needle. How could he fail to notice it when it was clearly protruding from the meter? This unfortunate misdemeanour by my sister resulted in poor Deborah receiving a black eye and a bust lip. It also had major impact for the family. The Scottish Electricity Board estimated the electricity used but not calculated and paid for. The household was then disconnected and we couldn't afford to pay the £200 fine. For us that truly was the Winter of Discontent.

After about a week or so living grimly on candles Aunt Elsie loaned my mum the money to get it re-connected. There was an agreement that she could pay it back weekly. Unfortunately the timing was not right as it coincided with Uncle Charlie being released from prison. The money intended for the electricity board's bank was spent on booze. It was whisky galore indeed.

Things didn't get any better. Our mother, who often in times of stress turned out to be violent, was even more prone to do so when she had a skin-full. She was constantly arguing aggressively with my father. Although father was a heavy drinker too his temperament was quite the opposite. A sweet natured chap, he unfortunately on this occasion rose to the bait and for his troubles suffered a broken ashtray in his face. I once tried counting the scars on his face. I gave up on that when I reached fourteen of them. That day, whilst father went off to hospital to get stitched up the rest of the family carried on with their jolly. None gave a flying thought to the likely effect such gratuitous violence and drinking might have on the children. In fact, they were inclined to not give a holy shit that they had left us kids in the dark with no electricity. As inconvenient there was the lack of a refrigerator, no television, in fact there was nothing. There are few places as soulless as a council flat without electricity.

A month was to pass before we as a family could flick the switch to put the lights and all else on. Only afterwards were we to learn that Uncle Charlie had spent six months banged up in Barlinnie, Scotland's most notorious prison. This nick had a reputation for holding the most feared, dangerous and vicious prisoners. One such was Jimmy Boyle. He had earlier slaughtered another gangster, hence his notoriety and long prison term in this grim Alcatraz of Scotland. Whilst imprisoned he had turned his hand to art and sculpturing. Boyle afterwards wrote a book, A Sense of Freedom, which so caught the public imagination that a movie was subsequently made of his criminal and prison experiences.

Our Uncle Charlie was a guest of – 'Her Maj', due to his having slashed someone's face: so he was not the nicest of men. You could say he was a pure bred bastard. Although I was very young at the time I recall how he had picked up a fire poker and struck Aunt Vera in her face with it. This was due to his frustration as there was no beer to hand. For some reason she stayed married and living with him for years. Then, one Christmas Day he just took himself off, out of the family home and walked into the River Clyde. The police and firemen dragged his body out later but there were no tears shed by me for Charlie. I was indifferent to his demise. The same couldn't be said for my mother. For mother, Christmases were never to be the same again. Little did we know that years later she would lose her son to the same ghastly fate.

Scotland has a reputation for celebrating New Year's Eve in style. From an early age we youngsters learned to bide our time until the oldies had a glow on. When they were distracted we would then sneak in and steal their beer. Back then a lot of the adults, mainly family, used to drink what was known locally as electric soup, which was Tennents Super Lager.; Strong for a beer, it is about 9% proof and a short-cut to drunkenness. Then the addled party voices would raise the rafters.

There were good parties in which there would be night-long singing and dancing. This would mostly be to country music or vogue singers like Dr. Hook. Invariably these parties ended up in arguments that spoilt the night's carousing. Mother used to say New Year's Eve was just an excuse for getting pissed. Why did they need such an excuse when they partied most nights anyway?

Routine returned after New Year. The school gates opened but not all the kids went through them. Quite often the children's mothers were so bladdered through drink that they could not raise themselves or their kids from their beds. When this happened we went to school in the afternoon and tried to pick up the pieces. We children were humiliated by this as her intention was hardly for us to get free dinners. Parents' thoughts were not altruistic. They were not thinking of improving their kids' education; they knew and we knew too that by going in late we would get our free school dinners. These would often be, if not the only meal of the day, the main meal of the day. A hot meal was something you couldn't count on when arriving home in the evening. Very often the fridge and cupboards were empty but of course there was always money for electric soup.

Auntie Katie sometimes visited and how we hated her doing so. Kate was so manipulative when it came to booze. All of my mother's side, bar two were alcoholics. Auntie Katie would arrive with maybe two cans of beer. These were described as 'just a little taster.' This small act of kindness wasn't without ulterior motive. This act of charity would be followed by a dirge explaining that she was out of money. She knew what she was doing. As soon as my mother tasted the beer everything else was out of the window.

Aunt Katie lived with my Gran as she needed such sanctuary from a violent relationship. The fact that grandmother's cupboards were never empty I should imagine was a factor too. There was never a thought given to the children's needs because she could be sure there would be more beer on its way. It is the way things were and for those of us who knew no better or knew similar families it was normal.

On those occasions we would have to wait until my

father turned up. On his arriving he would be furious to find Auntie Katie lying there on her chair. It got worse for there was often evidence that she had wet herself. No one sat on that seat due to the stink of urine that radiated from it. Having vented he would then send one of us to the chippie to fetch a couple of bags of chips and a loaf of bread. That was it. It was not much but we were grateful for it and rarely did dipped sandwiches taste so good.

At the time Aunt Katie was going through a particularly rough time. As kids we didn't realise the seriousness of it. It turned out that her daughter's boyfriend, when she was in a drunken stupor, had lured her into his house. This was situated next door to hers. Little did she realise his underhand motives. She realized his purpose after she had been beaten shit out of and raped. There was of course a trial but it all got pretty complicated.

The truth was that the boyfriend Davey had been beating up her daughter for years. Because my cousin was now in 'victim' mindset she didn't leave. At seventeen years of age she ended up preggers again just as her mother had done. The judge who presided over the case was pragmatic. He decided that because she knew of his violent nature she should not have entered the house. As she should have known better she was partly responsible. It got pretty much thrown out of court.

Throughout the trial my mother attended court to offer support for her sister. This meant we would be left babysitting. It also meant that after judicial proceedings had closed they would all go into a pub and they would stay there until towels were up.

In due course they received from the court the expenses claim for babysitting. This money was accepted as a sort of compensation and invested in another ritual and wearisome troublesome party. Such trials and tribulations were the rituals of our upbringing. After the ordeal of the court case the reason for it was never again discussed, at least not in front of the kids.

A few weeks passed and another family drama unfolded. My Uncle Pete was sent to London but the reasons for his exile were all very secretive. As far as we knew he went there looking for work. It was said that he was a Corgi-registered heating and plumbing engineer and there was little work available in Glasgow.

We then learnt that he had been exiled by my gran after being caught 'kiddie-fiddling'. Nothing else happened to him other than his public shame and exile. The matter was swept under the carpet. That was just the way things were handled back then.

After living for a year in London with my other London-based Uncle Pete returned. It materialised that he had been caught trying to get into bed with his charitable host's daughter. After a good and much deserved kicking Pete was put on a train back to my gran's. The matter was again dropped from conversations.

Our Uncle Pete took a shine to me but he never attempted anything. I did know of incidences like tit touching and bum patting but these happened to my sisters. Years later he was to endure a fatal heart attack. He was fifty-year of age at the time and was then living with his mum.

As the years went by my sister Deborah set her feet along a very destructive path. In order to feed her glue sniffing addiction she would rob and steal anything that wasn't nailed down. She came home late one night and there was a big tell-tale black ring around her mouth. She was spaced out of her head. My mother at the best of times was not particularly vigilant but she was that night. On seeing the state Deborah was in she punched my sister so hard that I swear her feet left the floor.

Little did mum realise that glue sniffing was the least of her worries. Deborah had always been rebellious and she was my father's favourite. The two of them would go out at night and steal whatever they could. This particular period marked the beginning of repeated police raids on our house. Deborah was expelled from school for turning up at school 'glued up' and what did she do, she promptly punched the gym teacher. Deborah had a loving temperament but it sometimes abandoned her; and her vicious temper would come into play. My father once returned home with boxes of food he and Deborah had stolen from a local store. By this time my brother was a member of this small band of not so merry men. I am not sure how dad knew we were due to be raided. Taking a Stanley knife he carefully slit chairs and sofa and placed all the stolen stuff in the sofa. We children then had to sit very carefully on the settee and easy chairs so that it appeared to be the perfect family home and for sure butter wouldn't melt in our mouths.

As expected, PC Plod and his little lot were soon pounding on the door following which our home was searched from top to bottom. To be truthful it didn't take them very long and there wasn't that much to it. Dad's ruse worked like a charm and the boys in blue left our flat empty-handed. We were all much amused by the way things had worked out.

Mother was completely in the dark as to what was going on. The only time she never had a drink in her was when she was too ill from retching. One day, out of the blue, my sister was put in a care home for badly behaved teenagers. Her glue sniffing by that time had escalated to cannabis. It progressed from that to what were called uppers-and-downers. These were made up of 'in-between', Valium, jellies and basically anything Deborah could get her hands on. My mother and I visited her in the children's home. Deborah told us that if asked if we want a cup of tea made by the inmates, to get a small reward; to say no. We would have gladly welcomed a cuppa but she warned us that entirely out of spitefulness the tea-makers would have almost certainly spat in the brew.

No question about it following that remark. We would not be accepting any such offer. It was horrible to see my sister in such an environment and that night I cried myself to sleep.

Around this time my brother Alfie was also heading down a very slippery slope. He had started to smoke dope and then moved on, as many do, to pill popping. Alfie had a lot of issues and things were going on in his life that had a major impact on him. Like Deborah; he was diagnosed as schizophrenic and he began receiving injections to help deal with the issues. It was sad to see him afflicted in this way because he too had a lovely disposition. His laugh was infectious but because of the behaviour-changing injections he was soon walking around hopelessly sedated and very much like a zombie. It seemed to us the cure was as bad as the ailment. Such was his behaviour that we never knew if he was popping or if it was the jag (injection). Unsurprisingly my brother and my sister would soon be receiving prison sentences courtesy of Her Majesty.

About this time there had been rumours in the area that one particular man was inviting children into his house. Following their entrapment and due to their vulnerability he would dope these kids with either drink or drugs and then molest them. Years were to pass before my brother, Alfie, confided in me what had happened to him. One evening when in the man's home he was passed out on the couch. When he awoke or rather gained consciousness he did so to find his trousers were around his ankles. It was very clear that he had been raped by the bastard He told us he remembered drinking beers, smoking pot and sniffing poppers before he passed out. My brother often wondered if this incident influenced his decision to become homosexual. Later he would rationalise the situation and decided it had not.

As children it was common for us to play in the back yards of the terrace houses. This involved jumping over the dykes and otherwise just messing around. It was on one of these innocent and happy occasions that we happened to peer through this pervert's windows. We couldn't believe what we were seeing but we couldn't disbelieve our eyes either. Our other friend, Jenny, was in the front room of this monster's house and we could see him bathing her. We kids banged hard on the room's window and we then ran off. When we later saw our friend we asked what was that all about she just replied they had no hot water at their home.

We thought that this was a strange answer but we never really gave it another thought. Perhaps, being children, we didn't consider the incident as other than a minor scandal. We were too young and innocent to realise that such a man was highly dangerous. He was the scum of the earth, another kiddie fiddler using his adult wiles to betray the innocent and the trusting: The lowest form of life.

Years later he would be found dead, stabbed to death in his own bed. As far as we were concerned it was good riddance to bad rubbish. What goes round comes round. This was karma at its best and poetic justice all in one so better late than never. After hearing from Alfie what had happened I had a deep heart-hatred for that excuse of a man, thankfully time has allowed me to move on.

Chapter 2
Alfie's Story

My brother Alfie didn't have a happy life at all. He was a very troubled young man, who throughout his short life was immature and vulnerable. Because of his tortured existence he was given to emotional outbursts. As my mother says, children learn what they live. Alfie could occasionally be very bad tempered. My younger brother would flare up over the slightest thing over what seemed to us to be trivial matters. It was the way he was, it was the condition he suffered from and there was little we could do about it except learn to live with it.

When my brother was seventeen years old he was caught doing a creeper. At least that is what they call it in the criminal underworld. To those of us better natured this weird activity was something that would appeal only to weirdos. In reality it was an odious criminal offence that was both disturbing and frightening.

Doing a creeper meant breaking into people's homes at night whilst they are asleep in their beds. Alfie often did these creepers when accompanied by his friend Tim. He had a strange sense of humour or devilment. Tim thought it quite a lark to piss on the bedroom floors of their unsuspecting victims. It was a sort of trademark; it was urine graffiti I suppose. Yes, Alfie was a very troubled boy. When finally caught carrying out such unsociable acts he was up before the beak and sentenced to six months imprisonment in Longriggend Remand Centre, situated in Upperton, Airdrie.

Longriggend is a Victorian prison building. As with most jails of that period this institution was extremely old and cold. Sanitation was not at its best and Alfie often complained about emptying the shit buckets and slopping out. He would often be heard to murmur, 'them are the rules. You won't beat them and you never get the better of the turnkeys.'

The institution, for want of a better word, was a prison in which drug abuse was widespread. In fact this was true of most of Britain's prisons that have been dubbed universities for criminals. It was generally assumed that much of the stash was brought in by the screws in an effort to calm down the inmates and make their own lives easier. The screws often turned a blind eye to drug related deals and misdemeanours. Again, it was anything for an easy life. I honestly cannot find it in my heart to blame them. In 2007 Longriggend Prison was demolished having then been described as 'a breeding ground for criminals' by Tom Buyers, the Scottish Prison Inspector.

Longriggend Prison riots, which Alfie took part in, earned him some recognition albeit of a notoriety kind. He was one of the muppets that sat it out on the prison's roof. Alfie never did learn his lesson in that supposed place of rehabilitation. Most of his buddies were junkies. His pill popping mates where all in there too. My brother never really got into trouble but I do know that he got a beating up whilst in there. At the time he was sharing a cell with my cousin Tim. This wasn't necessarily a good thing as, Alfie; he could talk for Scotland. As company he could be quite hard work at times. He is hyper-active, it is as though he's wired up like he's on speed. There is never a need for him to be on a substance as it was his nature to be hyper. It was about this time that Tim and Alfie fell out. We learnt that whilst Alfie was asleep in his cell bed and long after lights out Tim was up at the cell's barred windows hurling abuse at prison officers patrolling the courtyard below. The noise he was making had awoken Alfie. He unwisely went to the cell window to see what the commotion was all about. It was poor timing for, as his face appeared at the barred window, the floodlight held by the prison officers illuminated him. Let us say Alfie was over-exposed. He later explained to me that he then automatically began to dress himself. I was a bit confused by his telling me this: 'Why get dressed after lights out?' I asked him.

I was soon enlightened. He dressed himself knowing from previous experience that soon the keys would be heard turning in the cell door. By then he hoped to have as much clothing on as possible. The prison officers would pounce on him. He would then be dragged off to the segregation unit otherwise known as the 'seg'. There he would be used as a punch and kick-bag by the prison warders.

Although the offence had not been Alfie doing the shouting and abuse you still have to abide by the cons rules. Rule number one is no grassing, no informing on others. My poor brother kept his mouth shut and took his beating. It wasn't long before Alfie was banged up again. In his favour it must be said that he was never imprisoned for crimes of violence. One didn't need to be a graduate in rocket science to figure out why Alfie kept on getting collared as basically he was a shit criminal.

Another reason why he was caught so often was down to the fact that the poor soul was totally out of his face. Often he hadn't the foggiest idea what he had done until he found himself being awoken by policemen in his latest cell accommodation. By this time he was well known to the constabulary and they sort of sympathised and treated him well. They would tease him and then go through the usual routine of telling him not to come back. It was never going to be long before he was again their guest. Alfie had adopted the philosophy of 'can't do the time, don't do the crime.'

My brother's next little stint of incarceration was a one year sentence to be served in another Young Offenders Institution. Known as Polmont, the holding unit was not actually in that town but instead situated in Falkirk. I think this jail was a bit of a shock to Alfie's system as he didn't have the same inmates or warders as those in Longriggend Prison.

Polmont is Scotland's largest Young Offenders Institute. Like Longriggend Prison, drug abuse and violence was rife. On a few occasions Alfie had run-ins with little wannabe gangsters. As a consequence he picked up a few black eyes, broken ribs and on one occasion a broken wrist. Although Alfie had a quick temper he was neither aggressive by nature nor a natural fighter. Small in stature he made quite a tempting target for the bigger more aggressive bullies. He at sometime confided in me that in Polmont he had been somebody's bitch.

Alfie had never been involved with gangs. Although he hung around with a lot of mates, they didn't see themselves as a gang. They never went out looking for fights. On the contrary they avoided them and instead focused on small time opportunist thieving. In a word they were petty thieves. The motive was simple. They needed the proceeds of their thefts to pay for hash and lighter drugs. At this stage of their lives heroin and other hard drugs had never entered the picture. Alfie and his chums spent a lot of time in my sister Maddie's house. There they simply chilled as they listened to music whilst getting themselves stoned. They liked nothing better than to get hold of as much hash as they could get their hands on, smoke a few bongs and see which one would whitey first and then he would be slagged off. It was all done given and taken in good humour, just a wee bit of the old Glasgow banter.

One evening Maddie came home early and on coming into the living room could hardly see through the smog. It was so hazy in there that she at first thought a fire had broken out. Only then did she realise that there were a lot of bongs on the go. That place must have been absolutely toxic. Maddie was none too pleased when, much to everyone's amusement, the cat started to climb frantically up and down the curtains. As the cat was behaving so oddly Maddie started running around and flapping. Her behaviour to the assembled onlookers at least, was as bizarre as was the cat's behaviour. This bonus performance had them hooting with derision. Amidst the chortling could be heard Maddie plaintively crying, 'my poor wee cat, ya wee bastards.'

There was nothing wrong with the poor cat. It was simply stoned out of its mind, the same as the group was.

My sister Maddie is one of those trusting people who are very susceptible to suggestion. One Saturday night my sisters Shona and Maddie were having a little session with the boys; now Maddie doesn't smoke ganja, so she decided to deck a couple of jellies. Just as the buzz of the jellies was wearing off, Shona my sister gave Maddie a piece of Rizla cigarette paper and told her it was an acid. For the following three hours Maddie was telling all and sundry about the 'trails' and of how the trails were wonderful to watch; the power of suggestion indeed! She was very vulnerable and she swallowed without question anything she was told no matter how outlandish.

Shona never told the boys it was fake acid so they too thought Maddie was wasted and freaking out on the substance. The only one who knew that Maddie hadn't taken mind altering substance was Shona. I truly wish that I had been there.

All were content with what fate had doled out to them and none of Alfie's friends seemed to want to leave Glasgow. All were happy with their friends, their families and even the prisons. If they had any focus, at all, it was their constant pursuit of 'rock n' roll'. This was a euphemism for the dole, in other words state handouts. This form of income meant they could lie on their beds all day and be swag men at night. In this way, state benefits was actually breeding crime, it was fertilising the soil in which the ghost-class exist. None of the circle ever left Glasgow. There was no inclination for them to do so. They would live and die happy in this great Scottish city without any question. Placed in any other city or town, country or environment they would quickly succumb. The attrition rate was appalling. Little did we know at the time that out of twelve young persons in that group only one would survive?

After Alfie's detention at Polmont Young Offenders Institution the lad was considered to have graduated in the system's university of crime. He was now a fully fledged out of his head junkie with a penchant, if not a survival need, for committing petty crime. On his release from prison we held a party at my sister's house to welcome him home. By now it was obvious to all that Alfie was not the same person. My poor brother was by now hopelessly paranoid. So much for Britain's system of rehabilitation of young offenders!

My near demented sibling always used to get the giggles when smoking hash. After this further decline he seemed to think that everyone was laughing at him. We were blissfully unaware that he would often hear voices in his head. These were telling him to do 'bad things.' I never asked him to elaborate, I didn't have the heart and would there be any point. It would have only encouraged him.

When Alfie graduated at the ripe old age of twenty one he would find himself doing an unwelcome stretch in Barlinnie Prison. Longriggend and Polmont jails, whilst still hard places are like a walk in the park compared to the notorious Barlinnie Prison. It has been dubbed the San Quentin of Scotland. There could be found bad bastards galore. There were many tales surrounding Barlinnie Prison. One that sticks to this day in my mind was, when a brute of a guy with some cronies came into Alfie's cell and roughly demanded that he remove his trousers. This was my brother's first night in the jail. Naturally he thought he was about to be treated in a most unnatural way, that he was about to be gang raped. He later told me that he literally shit his pants. In truth these bad guys had no intention of molesting him for they just wanted his designer trainers. Perhaps such an approach amused them. It could have been worse than the loss of a pair of trainers. My brother had a lucky escape that night and how he knew it. Such things did happen to many unfortunates.

This awful prison was rife with drugs. It was no wonder that Alfie continued to use heroin or whatever his slender means could afford to buy. My mother often sent him money and on this occasion asked if me and my cousin Lanie would go to the prison to see Alfie. I had no qualms about visiting my brother; I just thought it odd that she wanted me to go with Lanie. On the bus to the prison my friend told me that she had with her a £20 wrap of heroin and £20 bit of dope. Lanie's intention was to pass it to Alfie via a kiss. My mother was very anti-drugs but anything to make her son's life a little better in that hell hole; and it was then that all of her principals went straight out the window.

Alfie told me that in Barlinnie you could buy a joint for two pounds. It was literally a cigarette paper with a bit of hash rolled up in it. Known as the Barlinnie Skinny it was better than nothing. By now Alfie was getting remedial treatment for his heroin addiction and had been put on Methadone. Methadone is a pain reliever and helps with the detoxification of the heroin. It takes the edge away and makes the withdrawals a little easier to bear. Methadone is supposed to be more addictive than heroin so whilst he was getting medicated with the Methadone he would still buy heroin. Alfie says most junkies hate methadone because it tastes like shit it can rot your teeth and is known as the 'green gunk'. When Alfie was inside we had a few other family members in there but they were in different units to Alfie so he didn't have much back up. After a few months in Barlinnie he was released and that was the last time the errant Alfie found himself at her Majesty's pleasure.

My father had little love, time or respect for my younger brother. I can't be sure but the root cause could have been family rumours that Alfie was not his biological son. It was said in Chinese whispers that my mother had an indiscretion with one of her sister's husbands. Biological father or not he liked nothing better than to treat Alfie like shite. He constantly dented the lad's confidence and it was quite sad to watch. Alfie, being the only son, wanted nothing more than to be loved and respected by his father. It was a futile hope for it never happened this side of his dying day. In fairness my father was not a pitiless man by nature. He was usually hard working and all things aside he was considered to be jovial. Sadly, Alfie's presence revealed a darker side to his character.

When this happened it was not a spectator sport and it was no pleasure to watch. I would always try to intervene to stop it happening if I was present. Father would encourage my younger sister Shona to play box with Alfie. Then, when the inevitable happened and Shona would be 'victim' of Alfie's reaction. It would not be long before she would start shrieking. Then father would hold Alfie down and let Shona beat seven bells out of him. So young, she was unaware that she was being cruel to Alfie and thought it was just a game and indeed fun.

Alfie would do all sorts of manner of things to impress my father and he did so behind my mother's back. There was no way she would have knowingly let him run wild and steal. Under his father's malign influence he would break into public telephone boxes. Then, quite cleverly and with the aid of a lollipop stick and a little chewing gum he would place the stick underneath where the coins drop and slowly and very patiently tease out the coins. He became quite adept at it and on a good day would empty the box. He said he had favourite boxes. In the run-up he kept an eye on how many people where using selected telephone boxes and that box would then be his target. In those days most people didn't have telephones in their homes and cell phones were the stuff of science fiction. This meant of course that public telephone boxes were kept quite busy. Some even had queues forming outside them. It was too bad if a pair of love-birds wanted to smooch the night away.

Cigarettes: Alfie would then buy himself a couple of 'singles', which was commonplace then. Most of the single cigarette buyers were children who lacked the money to buy them in packets. Usually my brother had some singles or, if it was a good day, he would treat himself to a packet. The rest of the money pilfered would be given to my father. Father could then go for a pint and taking the money offered by Alfie he would give him a kindly pat and murmur, 'thanks, son.' It was theatre. Father never showed any genuine gratitude for his son, bitterness was always just under a very thin skin. He never lost his loathing for poor Alfie.

My brother and his friend Tim once gave my father £50. It was part of the proceeds from their clambering up a builder's scaffolding and stealing lead from a roof. This was followed by a lull in hostilities and boxing matches were suspended for a couple of weeks. Who knows? Maybe there was just a little respect in dad's breast but if so it was kept very well hidden. No one would have envied Alfie's existence.

Alfie was destined to follow in my uncle's footsteps and his body would be eventually dragged from the River Clyde. Afterwards, my much abused brother was buried in a paupers grave months after having been reported missing. He had just seemed to vanish. He was last seen in November and reported missing in the January of the following year. It wasn't unknown for Alfie to take off and do a little sofa-surfing on a mate's couch or floor. Easygoing, he just went with the flow.

He had his moment of fame when he made an appearance in the Big Issue, the magazine for Britain's abandoned and homeless wanderers. He went off the radar in January and we were given the news of his body's recovery in June when he was found. He had spent all that time in the River Clyde and because of a police cock-up, it turned out had actually buried him in March, they had mixed up the DNA. It was bad timing. At the time Glasgow forensics was being moved to Dundee. This explained why Alfie's DNA was overlooked. It was a poignant ending to a very sad existence. Even in death he was not spared misfortune for he always said he wanted to be cremated. He was horrified at the thought of worms crawling over him. But, because he had been buried as a John Doe my mother felt it was too much for her to cope with if she was required to exhume his remains and to then burn them.

Chapter 3
The Agony and the Ecstasy

A few years before Alfie's death; my family had to endure the heartbreaking loss of my sister Deborah. She too had lived as a victim of circumstance. During her all too brief life with us she had a much troubled existence. Deborah was quite a spiritual young woman who insisted on attending Church most Sundays. She later confided that she was hoping God would get the devil out of her head.

As a teenager Deborah had spent most of her young life in and out of children's homes. My sister became so institutionalised that she stoically accepted her fate when she was sentenced to six months imprisonment in Cornton Vale, Scotland's only women prison. Deborah had been arrested for being drunk and disorderly. It was while she was being 'processed' at the police station that it was discovered that she had outstanding warrants and fines. This ensured her being sentenced to imprisonment.

Cornton Vale too is a very old prison and houses many violent females. It was as well that Deborah could stand up for herself that she experienced no real dramas whilst there. There were so many girls from the Children's Homes incarcerated in that prison that Deborah soon had plenty of friends. A likeable character; she told it like it was black is black, white is white, what you see is what you get!

Deborah was an enthusiastic reader so she read ceaselessly. Her passion for books helped to speed up the passage of time. There were drugs galore and she found a way to escape from her four brick walls of her cell in the form of jellies. There was only one occasion that Deborah felt she had put herself in a bit of a dodgy situation and could have come unstuck. At the time she owed one of the dealers some drugs money. The frustrated female dealer was threatening to let her have a shank (knife) in the ribs. Unfortunately for the dealer she picked on the wrong one. Deborah waited until the drug seller was alone and beat her so badly that her annoyer was hospitalised. That was the end of that matter and the debt was dropped. It was typical of the lawless jungle she inhabited.

Upon her release Debs went quiet for awhile. I think in her heart she wanted to slow down a bit and perhaps wipe the slate clean. In her mind was the desperate need to remove herself from temptation and make a fresh start somewhere. My sister had a friend who lived in Edinburgh. As she daydreamed about her best wishes she often talked of visiting her friend but for some reason never quite got round to doing so. I think it was because her family was her rock. She could not get the will to leave, even for a few days break.

Three months later Debs was again arrested for drunk and disorderly behaviour. On this occasion it was for fighting in the street and this time she was fined. Appearing before the magistrates the panel ordered that she pay the £200 pound fine. Failing this she would be returned to Cornton Vale for a fortnight. Where was a kid like Deborah going to find £200? The latter was her only choice and again the cell doors slammed behind the vulnerable kid. The prisons were Victorian, so were society's attitudes and responses to those who fell through the net.

This was a cycle that, in Deborah's case, was to be repeated on other occasions. Help was at hand and during one of the periods of her release, with the assistance of social workers and probation officers, Debs got a flat in the Gorbals district of Glasgow. Whilst she was living there my sister Shona and I would often visit. We were always well received and we three would sit for hour's playing cards, drinking cider and generally hanging out. These were the better memories of time spent with the unfortunate Deborah.

Then, out of the blue; Deborah returned home having surrendered her flat. When we asked her why she had done so, her reply was that she had a falling out with the neighbours. As she explained the circumstances behind her decision she seemed very agitated. I wondered if that wasn't due to her having upped her medication.

We were sitting quietly together one night and the conversation turned to what had really motivated her to move out of the apartment so generously provided for her. To my grave I will never forget what my sister told me. One evening, when sitting on her own in her little apartment, she heard her door being kicked in. Knowing Deborah was on her own, and vulnerable, five guys came in and attacked her just for the fun of it. They did it for the kicks they got out of it and there was much of that going on. Those guys beat her very badly and they then took it in turns to rape her. Still not satisfied with the brutishness they then, one by one, took it in turns to urinate over her. As they did so they took care to direct their streams of piss all over her face. They then stole what few belongings she had and then, for good measure, one shit on her floor much to the mirth of this hideous gang. All of them were high on jellies.

I asked her why she never reported the rape and all else that had happened to her. She replied very calmly -

'what can be done?'

It was not a question but it was a simple statement. I instinctively knew that she knew some of the perps but was far too savvy or scared to go naming these guys. The gang that had committed this awful series of crimes were evil, through and through, and were often a law unto themselves. Deborah left her little home where she had been so disgustingly defiled that same night. My sister came to my mother's in the morning after having wandered the bleak streets in the pouring rain and darkness. Whist aimless wandering, she had been in a trance.

After some months things seemed to be getting better for Deborah; sure, she was still on heavy doses of prescribed drugs whilst self medicating. However, she seemed more hopeful and happier that she now had a job. She loved children and Deborah had always dreamed of being a nursery nurse. Such a career, at least for the time being, wasn't achievable due to her medication, her responses, were a little too slow. She did get a job as a volunteer. This was working for a local charity called 'Gingerbread' that helped children from under privileged families. My sister seemed to be doing so well and it was heart lifting to see her optimism and endless faith in the goodness of human nature in spite of all she had suffered. Regrettably this little stint of happiness was to be short lived. We were soon to discover why when PC Plod appeared at the door. He was there to let my mother know that Debs was in the Victoria Infirmary. The poor girl, for reasons known only to herself, led her to make a futile attempt on her own life with the help of a razor blade.

This was the third time that she had attempted suicide. On the first occasion it was more of a cry for help and done on impulse when she threatened to hurl herself from a high rise. After some reasoning by a kindly policeman she had been talked out of her folly. Upon their reaching the ground the cop who had rescued her arrested her for the misdemeanour known as a Breach of the Peace. You just couldn't make up such mindsets. It leads you to wonder just who was the most disturbed, the distressed rejects of society's failings or the same society's support system workers.

On the second occasion my lovely but unfortunate sister chose a concoction of pills and Vodka. Deborah was certainly a tormented soul. The family was shocked by this latest attempt at taking her own life. It was bad enough with the booze and pills episode but this was a whole different league. What were her demons, her extremes of distress that she would go to such lengths to make a conscious decision to go towards the light?

My sister and I visited her in hospital but mother point blank declined to go. Despite having delivered five children in hospital mother had an abnormal fear of the place. I imagined that, as she became older, she saw hospitals as being less for the living but more of hospices. In her mind hospitals had become places for the dying.

My father had been to see Deborah the previous evening. He had taken her the usual hospital gifts. There were the grapes, flowers and he had been thoughtful enough to include a get well card. Personally I thought his doing so a little bizarre considering her motivation for her failed attempt to take her life. However, I appreciated the thought behind it and I am sure my sister did too.

I am not a big fan of hospitals either. I found visiting hours awkward and boring. Our first sight of Deborah was her lying there with her lower arms tightly bandaged.

My poor sister was still under heavy sedation. I can't be sure if she was aware of her situation or of whether she was coming or going. After a few endearments my sister Shona and I retreated to the vending machine. As we took our leave we each kept our thoughts to ourselves. What was there to say? In a family like ours you think you have seen it all and then something like this happens. Only then do you realise that you don't know the half of it.

When we returned to my sister's bedside, each with our small plastic beakers of hot tea, Deborah seemed a bit more compos mentis; although clearly sedated. She was aware of our presence but none of our small group could find words to say. We three just sat in stony silence with our own thoughts until the nurse told us visiting time was over. When we waved our goodbyes to my errant sister there was a sense of relief that she was in good hands and physically recovering. On the other hand we had no idea what was going on in her disturbed mind.

On her release my troubled sister was met by Shona and I at the hospital. As part of her treatment Deborah was to receive counselling. It was then thought that, as she was clearly troubled, it would be better for her to undergo psychiatric assessment. It was suggested to my sister that she go there the following day after spending a little time at home in the company of her family. Little did we realise that as a voluntary in-patient she would be sectioned.

So this was the beginning of many visits to Leverndale Psychiatric Hospital. This institution is situated on Glasgow's south side. Like so much else of the Victorian era it is a depressing place, even to visit. What it must be like to be confined there hardly bears thinking about.

Shona and I visited Deborah with our eldest sister Madeline. As we sat waiting to be admitted to see our stricken sibling we could only take in the bleakness of our surroundings. This latest development was something none of us had been prepared for. We never before had reason to visit a Dickensian' asylum. For us two this was a whole new and unwanted experience. Bedlam updated. Men and women, who clearly weren't on this planet, were just wandering around in their night clothes. It was as clear as a pikestaff that they were all heavily sedated. There was something nightmarish about the entire spooky place. It was far worse than the movie, 'One Flew over the Cuckoo's Nest'. The institute's atmosphere and surroundings remind us of that movie and the other movie, 'The Walking Dead'. This asylum was indeed like the place of the living dead. People, strangely like zombies, were wandering about. They were physically present but their minds had gone. It was the most sobering and thought provoking experience either of us had ever encountered.

As we two waited we took it all in. I supposed we two sisters were entertained in a morbid sense by our surroundings and the patients. As we did so my sister Maddie spotted an old flame of hers. It was a moment of truth as she had earlier remarked when talking of the relationship that she'd had a lucky escape. Under the circumstances one could hardly argue with that point of view. Deborah was a no show that visiting day. She had decided she did not wish to come out of her room. She had told the nurse that she was just too tired from the effects of the medicines she had been given.

Chapter 4
Maddie's Story

Maddie was something of a tom boy and a loner. She disliked school intensely. The model of dumb insolence; she was unresponsive when attending and so unsurprisingly was still largely illiterate. She was later to be diagnosed as dyslexic. Knowing this, what torments she had endured at school hardly bears thinking about. Back in those days the condition of dyslexia wasn't recognised and affected pupils were dismissed as lazy, uncooperative or just damned brainless. In our family it was a running joke that if you sent Maddie to the corner shop for a pint of milk she would return with a loaf of bread.

Painfully unaware of her condition, only now can we appreciate the effects of the condition on her; it will have damaged her self esteem. Maddie was called many uncomplimentary names. Their meaning served only to reinforce the family impression that my sister was completely dumb. Bless her, she took it all in her stride and always laughed the insults off. Only with the benefit of hindsight can we appreciate that it was us being dumb and it was never her at all.

Verbal abuse was nothing new in our family. Everyone was on the receiving end of sharp tongues. Often it would be undeserved as the mouthy offender was just venting their frustration. Quite early on, Maddie began to feign stomach aches. These would have confounded medical science as they invariably occurred on Mondays. It suited mother because my sweet natured sister could be otherwise engaged helping mother to clean the family home. The reason my sister saw this as a satisfactory compromise was because she was so unhappy at school. The teachers were constantly mocking and humiliating my sister. They would make her stand up to read. She did this so badly that as she did so the classroom pupils joined in the chorus of derision. Maddie's absence from school was soon commonplace and it was not long before a truant officer was sent to our home to sort things out.

That minor council official would become a regular visitor to our home. There were the usual chats of, what is your problem? Was it a school or home problem? Maddie instinctively knew there was no way she could confide in him and express her feelings about home life. In our family you learnt from early on that it was best to keep your thoughts to yourself and especially so where authority was concerned!

Under pressure to do so Maddie, did reluctantly return to school. However, it was only a matter of time before things returned to normal. She was soon the Cinderella again and life just went on and on in its own fashion. She was very much a private person. When with my mates I did see her at school she would smile, she would pass the usual pleasantries and then quickly go on her way. For Maddie, being on her own was her preferred choice.

I don't think my sister was on her own because she had an unpleasing personality: far from it. Whatever, between her home and school life, her confidence, must have plummeted; Mother was too distracted by our own pressures to consider anyone else's demons and so life went on and tediously on. Some of us siblings were in a zombie kind of limbo. None of us noticed or cared that on many occasions Maddie felt the wrath of mommy dearest. This was because she was a habitual bed wetter and had been so from when she was tiny. My father would wake her up during the night in an effort to help her keep her bed dry. This avoided the mantra doled out if she wet her bed: 'You fucking pished yourself again!' This was invariably followed by a back-hander across her wee small face. It wouldn't be the first time my sibling would feel the consequences of finding her bed sheet saturated in her own urine. As a consequence she was increasingly agitated.

As a family we lived fairly close to Queens Park. It is a most beautiful recreational area. The park attracts families in the summer who go there to have picnics, to enjoy boat rides and take part in a score of outdoor activities including sports. It was a very popular day out, especially on the few occasions that Glasgow saw sunshine. Then everyone was certain to take advantage of the decent weather and folk would make a beeline for the park. The children would collect our soft drink bottles, usually the Irn Bru brand, which we called glass cheques. These bottle empties would be returned to the shops as they were recyclable and we would collect a few coppers on each returned bottle in return for our doing so. This money was as quickly converted to ginger, which is Glaswegian for juice, and of course sweets.

I recall my mother and Aunt Katie taking us to Queens Park for an afternoon's picnic. The occasion merited Katie's kids being with us. We children thought this was at least a one-off nice day. We had never been anywhere except once to Ayr. This is a seaside resort which we had visited on a day trip and that could have ended better than it did. On the day we visited Queens Park, Katie disappeared from the park early in the day. To us it was apparent where she had skulked off to when she returned with her bag filled with beer from the local off licence.

As soon as the other kids spotted her and heard the dreaded sound of the ring pull we knew the day was over. I can't say we were not disappointed or horrified. Unfortunately it was what we had become used to. Life was a constant series of disappointments. Promises in our families did not mean a thing. It is said, don't make a threat or a promise to a child you can't keep. Well, that little gem of a rule never applied in our home. It was not long after she had returned and the dregs of the electric soup went down that we had to put the pair of them in a taxi. By that time neither my mother nor Katie could stand properly. There was one little problem which was to remain our secret. The last thing we wanted the cab driver to know was that the hapless two had again soiled themselves.

Queens Park was an escape for Maddie too. She would seek solace there and amuse herself with her football and skateboard. In fact, left to her own devices, she was quite talented and could do keepie ups with the best of them. My sister knew lots of skateboard tricks. Maddie was always a quick learner apart from the problems normally associated with dyslexia. After a brief trip to Queens Park, she knew she would soon be looking into her mother's demonic eyes. This would happen upon it being discovered that my sister had not bothered staying home or going to school. Instead she had practiced her skateboard skills in the park. The outcome was that the truant officer had spotted her and reported Maddie to the social services. As an upshot of this, today was not going to be a good day. On this occasion we were all sitting at the table supping homemade soup. Luckily for us my mother had been having a few alcohol free days and was playing the domesticated busy bee. That was when the door shook from an authoritative rapping. This heralded an official is at the door. The one saving grace on this gloomy occasion was mother being sober. We were soon to realise that it was the social workers from Social Services doing the door rapping.

We kids practically broke our necks as we listened in to hear the conversation at the doorstep. There was little need for us to do so for by now the local authority officials were entering our home. Now don't get me wrong, this was not our first encounter with the SS. However, it did seem strange that the functionaries were here over something as trivial as Maddie playing truant. My sister hated school, end of. It was hardly a capital offence and she was hardly the first pupil to feel that way about her schooling.

Obviously the jobsworths didn't see matters in the same light as we did. They went though the usual mantras. All the insincere pleasantries were expressed when their body language was saying the opposite. Such officials have no desire to sit on the couch watching the family play at being the Walton's. They far prefer cutting it short, sloping off and dealing with their own dysfunctional families.

On that occasion there hadn't been any beer in our home for days. In fact the household was calm and there hadn't been a single drama of note. In this respect their visit was fortuitously well timed. It was amusing for us to watch my mother's acting skills. Oh, mother would have put Meryl Streep to shame. She was so surprised and concerned that our Maddie had been dodging school. No doubt she was inwardly seething that her errant daughter had chosen to spend her time on her skateboard instead of being at home with a mop in her small hands.

As we listened we could see mother's mind ticking over. We children were under no illusions. Each one of us knew that Maddie was really in for it after this theatre was over. My sister just sat there and was very composed throughout her ordeal. Maddie nodded approvingly very much and reminded us siblings of one of those ornamental dogs once fashionably placed in the backseat shelves of cars.

Mother was pure theatre and she was making all the right grunting noises. She knew the game as well as the town hall functionaries did. This was real life soap opera. Eventually mother pacified our unwelcome visitors. She told them what they wanted to hear and after going through the usual pleasantries the inquisitive interrogators went on their way. As a family we didn't want these types of officials interfering. We saw it as a small victory that they were finally gone, at least for the time being. For all our family's faults and here were plenty of them; we would prefer to have stayed where we were - than be placed in the hellish Social Care system. Better the devil you know than the devil you do not.

Our school friends never got to see our immaculate little house. There was a reason for this. You could not invite friends in case mother was having an off day and when at school we children didn't have crystal balls. Then there were other days best not mentioned and besides they were unlikely to appreciate mother's sense of humour. If my mother was sober at the start of a session she could be very good company. She had a very funny wit and was far from being ignorant. She was, despite appearances, well read and she was an avid viewer of the more serious documentaries. From her comments we knew that she was well informed.

Considering she does not exactly interact much with the outside world she is pretty well versed. Yes, the start of such homely little sessions was invariably harmonious and endearing. Then soon afterwards the booze bedded in and what a different tale to tell then. Mother's sense of humour evaporated. She would snap, become hostile and it was for us high time for a quick exit.

Many, well, the majority of people would describe Maddie as gullible and wouldn't be far wrong. In truth the poor and lovely girl was just too trusting. She was a great foil for my family's off-beat sense of humour. Typically, mother would send my sister to the shop to ask for a tub of elbow grease. The poor innocent never cottoned on to abuse of her naivety. Her innocence was irresistible for jokers. Father, when asked what colour he had in mind when painting, explained to her that he would be needing tartan paint. It was a shame they hadn't invented it for that would have wiped the smirk from his face. Maddie did have the loveliest of dispositions. She never took offence and she laughed as heartily as any of us did. We could all have learnt lessons from the lovely child.

As she grew up Maddie started to let her hair down a little. She lived and loved a lot and she was in her natural habitat when she got word of an all-night party. Mother's objection to such pursuits was mild theatre. She never really objected too strongly because most of the parties my sister attended were at my cousin's home. I suppose it was a rare occasion to be comforted by the thought that being family there would be no dramas to disturb her own sleep.

It did not quite go that way, one late night I heard a commotion in the back yard and tentatively opening the curtains I peeked out. There was our Maddie inelegantly clambering over the backyard fence, her dress hiked up.

My sweet sister was doing a runner from a cab driver who had indulged her whim to return to her home. At that unforgettable moment I guessed he might be regretting his small act of unwanted charity.

Maddie never cared for nicotine so wasn't interested in hash. It wasn't a moral decision as Maddie did adopt a taste for speed. She was introduced to the whizzy stuff, also known as the poor man's coke, through an old friend at a party. It worked for her. She was lively for a straight two days and didn't she just love the feel of it.

Taking it didn't harm her maternal instincts; No, not our Maddie. As she matured, if that is the right word in this context, my sister took on the mini-mum mantle. Maddie assumed responsibility for house cleaning and some family cooking. Not having a washing machine Maddie could be found most Sundays down at the laundrette doing what you do in such places, nattering away while the machines did your work. On occasion Shona and I would be there with her, just to hang out and help with the sheet folding, which for her, had to be just so. Having found the confidence that comes from such small freedoms Maddie wanted to spread her wings and live life a little. I think in hindsight that there was probably a wild side to my errant and very sweet sister. You can't imagine the relief she felt when she earned her one-way ticket out of the school gates one effervescent day. That was when she was about fifteen-years of age but who is counting.

Chapter 5

No one spanks Frank!

In the more relaxed environment of our cousin's home the weekends were something of a free-for-all. Think 'Drop-In Centre' and the right pictures will come into your mind. It suited Aunt Jackie, whose family instincts held that they were safer where she could keep an eye on them. To her way of thinking it was better than having them 'wandering the streets.' I am sure she had a point.

What passed for music, for this bunch was hardly the epitome of good taste, would be soon raising the rafters and there would of course be a ready supply of drugs. Aunt Jackie had three children, Andrea, Stuart and Mickey. Andrea was nineteen and had recently become a mum. Her partner of four years was still on the scene and Andrea was besotted by her latest paramour. At six feet and five inches tall it had to be admitted that Frank had plenty of presence and he was also very easy on the eye. He had turned a few maidens and not so maidenly heads. Putting it Andrea's way Frank was 'eye candy.' It got better for Frank had a keen sense of humour. They say that the quickest way to get a woman into bed is to make her laugh. There was no dour Scot about her boyfriend Frank. However, what did it for Andrea was that Frank actually had a job. True, he was a rarity who had not been fathered by the state.

On leaving school her boyfriend had whatever it takes to be taken on by a local firm as an apprentice stonemason. These craftsmen weren't badly paid and he was no exception. With an eye to the future it was in

Andrea's scheme of things to get hitched and live a fairy tale life with her Frank. It had never entered her head to marry or even consort with someone on social security known colloquially as doleys.

No way, Jose! Andrea wanted social status, conformity and security, Frank promised both. By now he was no stranger to her household. He had for some time been good mates with Andrea's brother, Stuart. They had been chums from their primary school days. Due to his height he was referred to as Big Frank. Andrea from the outset had her eyes and her fluttering heart set on Frank. It was a genuine affection. Her adoration of him never wavered. Andrea loved and appreciated the guy and had done so for years. In her parlance they were made for each other. Frank was two years her senior.

Being part of the furniture it was fitting that Andrea surrendered her maidenly purity on a time-honoured piece of the apartment's furniture. We never asked such a delicate question. It was assumed for no other reason than it being the most likely place, or otherwise it had been the uncarpeted floor. Soon after this hopefully happy occasion Frank and Andrea became each other's item. No slouch on the couch, Andrea tried desperately and persistently to get herself preggers. She had her naïve strategy well thought out.

Over the years the smitten kitten had become close to my mother. Although my aunt Jackie was liberal minded, for some reason, Andrea felt that she could confide better in my mother. What the foolish girl didn't know was that when mother indulged in a few libations with Aunt Jackie she would betray Andrea's confidences.

My mother would later tell me that Andrea had come to her on at least three occasions with pregnancy scares.

Mother was no fool and knew the only thing Andrea was scared of was not being pregnant! The poor girl must have been demented. To her way of thinking, if she and big Frank had a child, then entrapped he would be obliged to be hers for life. Fail! She was wrong very wrong on every level.

The first problem was that nurturing a small baby Andrea couldn't carry on partying. That sort of thing was now out of the window. She had a mother's responsibilities and my aunt Jackie was forthright on this point. As far as Aunt Jackie was concerned her own days of mothering where over and she now had her life back. Unprepared to be lumbered, even as a babysitter with Frank and Andrea's child; she made that sparkling clear to her daughter.

Jackie had raised her children with little or no help. None of the children's fathers had shown much interest in their progeny. The beaus can walk away from their trysts but mothers cannot. Years later Aunt Jackie would tell that when Andrea confided in my mother the news about the pregnancy from that moment on she had felt abandoned: The best laid plans of mice and men. Andrea had felt betrayed by the pregnancy as it began to slowly dawn on her that the better life she wanted for their child wasn't as enthusiastically endorsed by Frank. It was a moment of truth. Instead of the birth bringing the two closer together, as she had fondly imagined, she realised that her relationship was not as close as she believed and there were a few tears shed.

Baby Amelia was now on the scene and Big Frank was not on the radar screen as often as he once was. As the penny dropped the heated debates started. It was not long before Andrea realised that being saddled with a baby at such an early age was not going to be quite the pram walk in the park she had imagined it to be.

Dream on! Andrea had been hoping for conventional family life. She hadn't known her own father very well and she had most of all wanted things to be so different for baby Amelia. By painting Frank into a corner she was having the opposite effect to the one intended. In doing so she was pushing him away and it was destined to be a long way away. He had his heart set on London.

Having been caught in a love trap Frank would do one. Sadly, before his doing so he would make Andrea's life a pretty shit one. From the time of Amelia's birth he began to spend less time with her and his daughter. Sure, he would often brag about his beautiful child. Certainly he did all the right things by way of contributing to the costs of her upbringing. Alas, he showed no interest in spending time with the mother or their child and that upset Andrea. Her brother Stuart was happy to have his best mate back in the fold. Little did he know that their long term friendship would one day come into question?

Andrea by now was not getting on at all with Frank. Besides that, to make matters worse and her future less secure, she was unaware that her lover was having his cake and eating it. Frank would be up an attractive girl's skirt faster than a rat going up a drainpipe. When his two-timing nature came to Andrea's notice she would scream at him, telling him he was a big dirty cheating bastard. She was not far wrong in that observation. These set-tos led to violence and on each occasion the so-called love of his life would find herself on the receiving end of a couple of Frank's vicious backhanders. This behaviour was something that her brother Stuart was unaware of. Andrea was too ashamed to tell anyone about the violent nature of their relationship. It was all hushed under the carpet and everyone hoped that it would all blow over and the two, or rather three, would settle their differences and settle down. It was the way things were dealt with in my family.

Years later; the warring couple would find themselves locking horns in court in a custody battle. Such things are never pleasant experiences and can so easily become a clearing house for the resentment and anger of both parties involved. They are often opportunity to vent all pent up frustrations that underlie a failed relationship. Bitterness soon set in. Frank was to tell the court that Andrea was an unfit mother and in no state to look after his daughter. The struggle for custody would open up a whole can of worms. It materialised that not only had Frank beaten his betrothed up on several occasions, he had on one occasion poured scalding kettle water directly onto her back. This was whilst he was on one of his paranoid come-downs. No one, until the hearing, had any idea that their relationship was that volatile. Even Aunt Jackie was shocked. It was hard to believe that Frank, whom she had accepted as a member of her family, could be so callous and vicious towards her daughter. Frank had fooled some of the people some of the time but you can't fool all of the people all of the time. During the court proceedings he was exposed in his true light.

Because of the nature of his stonemasonry work Frank had good disposable income. A huge chunk of this was in the keeping of Andrea's other brother, Mickey. A quick thinking opportunist, he was thought of as a Mini Soprano. This is Glasgow slang for being a smart ass.

Andrea's brother had his finger in a few pies. In one of them he pulled out his thumb and goodness gracious me, a few wraps of the white powder emerged. It appeared that Frank had been preoccupied for it was learnt that somewhere along the line if; that is an appropriate term in this context, he was smoking cocaine. Like a lot of Mick Jaggers (junkies) the errant lover boy started off snorting. We were under no illusions and we all knew that was the beginning of a predictable outcome. That slippery slope was accelerating. Frank, sooner or later would become another statistic. He would prematurely take his dirt nap and he would never see his daughter graduate from university that was for sure.

During their court room confrontations Frank accused Andrea of being addicted to prescription drugs in the form of Prozac. Prozac was mainly prescribed as an anti-depressant, which Andrea needed for her anxiety and nerves. The Social Security was now in the family loop and they were doing routine background checks. It was a no-brainer anyway. The magistrates ruled that it would be in the best interests of Amelia if she remained in the care of her mother. Frank made the smart choice and never pursued the matter. In truth he had neither inclination nor intention to keep his daughter; he just wanted to hurt Andrea. If this was his purpose he achieved his goal.

The judicial upheaval and the stress would take their inevitable toll on the young mother. She suffered much pain from recurring kidney infections, migraines and nervous stress. For a short time, Aunt Jackie, whether she wanted to or not would be Amelia's primary carer. She had little choice for Andrea was battling her own demons and the side effects of Prozac. By this time the poor young mother was just another Prozac zombie and a heavily perspiring one too. Andrea did not get her fairy tale ending but as a form of compensation she would get to see her daughter graduate after successfully going through university.

Life goes on in its usual colourful way. The life cycle would begin again and it did so for Amelia. Andrea was destined to be a grandmother before she reached the forty years of age. Not surprisingly her brother Stuart and boyfriend Frank were never close - after all the nasty business at the custody hearing. This was when Stuart learnt the truth of Oscar Wilde's maxim: 'True friends stab you in the front.'

Chapter 6
Priestly Chastisement

Stuart busied himself with his other China's. His friends had always been a tight knit little crew that worked and played hard. They had hung out since they could venture out from their homes. Being born into the drug culture they enjoyed nothing better than getting wasted. This started when Stuart had begun to steal the weed that Aunt Jackie had been growing. These kids were street-wise and immediately recognised the leaf and anyway, Stew-Boy was a big Bob Marley fan. For years Aunt Jackie had explained to them that she was innocently growing tomato plants. Of course she tried to cover her small infamies up. She would go as far as buying vine tomatoes and pretend they had come from the plant. As the years went by the kids grew wiser and she was eventually sussed.

That cycle of life would then begin with a grim inevitability. The youngsters would start with the hash and then graduate to the University of Hard Stuff. Most of those in Stuart's small circle of friends had left school and were by this time working. Stuart had worked in the Spar eight-till-late store since he was fifteen years of age. He had begun as a shelf-stacker working on Saturdays and had worked his way up the small career ladder to become assistant manager.

Pretty much most evenings were spent with their chilling in Stuart's room. Been there, done that, it was the usual scenario that I was very familiar with. Bongs and doobies, it was only a matter of time before they felt the need to experiment and they did that in fine Glasgow style. The group started with Diazepam, better known as

Valium or blues. They then moved on to Jelly Babes, the street name for Temazepam. This substance is produced as a gel-filled capsule and taken orally. A normal therapeutic dose would be 10mg - 30mg following which you may feel less anxious and become relaxed and sleepy. At higher doses the effects of this substance are similar to those of alcohol. This is when you begin to feel less inhibited towards others.

It can alter your behaviour. In my experience people using Tems become talkative or over-excited. It can also lead to feelings of hostility whereas the user shows signs of aggression and their judgement is impaired. The effect of taking Tems is it can give you a false sense of confidence and in extreme cases cause you to believe you are invincible or invisible. Temazepam at one point was the most widely abused drug in Scotland and produced in a gel-type substance to discourage injection. However, as is so often the case, junk heads found a way round it. Heat it up really hot then suck it up into a pin and slam it in a vein as quick as possible before it cools and solidifies.

In theory great stuff except this is when it starts to solidify in the user's veins and then leads to rapid vein loss and abscesses. As a consequence many users moved the entry point to their groin (femoral) vein. They hit it up there, which is easier to begin with as you can use a thicker needle. This doesn't block as easily. It isn't the answer, think frying pan fire. The user then gets deep vein thrombosis (DVT) in the leg. This either develops into gangrene or ends up as an amputation. If you pull the short straw of life and death the hapless hooked user dies from section of a blood clot breaking off and blocking the heart or lungs.

These little yellow eggs caused much pain and

suffering. Scotland was to gain a reputation for having more than its fair share of amputees. The thing I never got about jellies, and I can remember asking Alfie what was the big thing about them, why where they so popular? He explained that the secret of jellies is in the fighting to stay awake. So I say; 'So you take a drug meant for sleeping and you then fight to stay awake?'

'Yeah,' he agrees.

'Why bother?'

He laughed and shrugged but I was none the wiser. This then was the chosen buzz for our small party and a lot of their fellow Glaswegians. Stuart and his buddies progressed to speed bombs. These would usually be wrapped in a cigarette paper and swallowed. This was a period when Maddie would enjoy the whizzy whizzy and she too, later on in life, would be hooked and become a complete speed freak. She would often tell me of her major come-downs. These included intense feelings of anxiety, extremely lethargy and paranoia. On some really heavy come-downs she would hallucinate. She described it as a Smith's album, you know really depressing.

Stuart's friend Andy was the first person and in fact the only person I knew who injected speed. I was aware of people injecting heroin but I had never heard of anyone doing it with speed. Andy had a really annoying speech impediment, a stutter like he had tourette's syndrome. It was like he was thinking too quickly and his mouth didn't, wasn't, able to keep up with his mind. He would speak in a hyper frenzy and was usually annoyingly repetitive. I tended to give him a wide berth. He was always on the shots. These ranged from an average of half a gram up to half an 8-ball (it's approximately an eighth of an ounce 3.5 grams of speed). Andy was completely bang on it. Most of the time he wore long sleeves this was a ploy to hide the track marks. He didn't fool anyone but himself as to everyone it was obvious why he was hiding his arms. Even in summer he never wore a T-Shirt. I think he was ashamed. Mind you, it's like that old joke: 'When is the Scottish summer? - That would have been last Wednesday!'

It wasn't uncommon for junkies to wear sleeves, they who wanted their failings to go unnoticed. Many years later Andy would successfully go through rehab. By that time he had practically run out of veins to jack up. He developed deep vein thrombosis through injecting in his groin. This was commonly associated with blood poisoning. Admitted to hospital he was delirious with a horrendous fever and unable to walk. Giving him IV antibiotics for two weeks they then administered it through a cannula inserted into his foot. This was necessary because there was no other useable vein on his body. Following this he had to self-administer heparin (anti-coagulant) injections in his stomach twice daily for about six months from there on.

Andy chose his future and he chose life. He did get cleaned up and he then found God. In later years he told me that he would continue to suffer flashbacks. These were unpredictable episodes of psychosis, acute paranoia, and manic depression. That by the way was on a good day!

Sadly, Lucifer prevailed and gave Andy a helping hand to the exit. All the suffering was to begin again and he surrendered to temptation. Poor Andy was to have his final fix before checking into the wooden Waldorf. Hopefully he had a rendezvous with Saint Peter. Surprisingly for Glasgow the weather on the day of his funeral was sublime. Basking in the warmth of the sunshine respects were paid for Andy. He had not always been a rattler and he was best remembered for the times when things were simply a little weed and life was joyous. I didn't attend the funeral but it was clear that he had a good send off and then Andy was no more. RIP Andy.

For a while, life for Stuart and his little band of smack heads ticked on by until they weren't getting quite the same buzz from speed and the speed bombs. It was then they discovered ecstasy. Dubbed x, it was then the new in-drug. Other than Ecstasy it was known as disco biscuits, smarties, doves; there were so many names for the love drug. When taking Ecstasy Stuart said he felt totally elated and was at one with the world. This was because the chemical release from the Serotonin it produces gives a feel good factor to the brain. He would get an almost Woodstock vibe; Peace brother.

It was when his friends were in his room chilling that a massive vibe would consume them. They would then declare that they all felt euphoric and spiritual. It never occurred to any of them that there was any harm in their new found passion. It didn't help that the logo on the substance was a little smiley face. The lethal drug has an aphrodisiac impact inducing horniness in many E-takers. Ecstasy-related deaths as news stories had surfaced in the media and in some respects those individual tragedies probably saved thousands of lives. People were now better informed about the importance of keeping themselves hydrated. There is always an opportunist and the price for a bottle of water in clubs went through the roof.

There are with most drugs common side effects. Common is the paranoia on a comedown, insomnia, fatigue, depression, jaw soreness from grinding. It is usual for drug takers to grind their teeth and is a habit horrible to watch. After watching those recovering from a heavy partying weekend you could see the drug had taken its toll on Monday mornings. One could be sure there wouldn't be much work done and like the Boomtown Rats they didn't like Mondays either.

Most of our cousins were of similar age and all knew each other well. Aunt Jackie had a far more relaxed attitude and her kids could talk to her about anything or so she thought. You would never in a million years go and ask for advice on sex or drugs in my home; as to do so was unthinkable.

Jackie was the youngest of my mother's sisters and a bit more with it. She was only sixteen-years old when she had to go and give my gran the good news. She was pregnant and the father was a Pakistani. No worries, as it was alright because if she changed her religion to Muslim they could get married.

Poor Jackie thought she had all the answers and to her the relationship and pregnancy was no biggie. Well, I thought my gran would combust. Oh how she freaked out. Talk about blowing a gasket. Just like a cartoon character there were vapours pumping from her ears. I think for a minute my gran thought she was sharing the room with Beelzebub. There was not enough Hail Mary's or Acts of Contrition in the world to help her out on this scandal. She knew well that reinforcements would have to be brought in.

'A bloody rag head, change your religion to bloody Muslim and shame my family by bringing a bastard desert-rat into this world and my family? Yes? And that will be the day when hell freezes over!'

Now my gran was not really known for her patience and she had a vicious razor sharp tongue. They were the days were you could speak without all that political correctness nonsense and she called it like she saw it and did not mince her words. She would constantly use expressions like 'play the white man' meaning play fair. If you ever said 'something was not fair' she would retort, 'What, darkies hair?'

She had no qualms about calling Pakistanis - Joes. This was a shortened form of Joe Daki - Paki. She loved listening to what she called nig nog jokes. This was the way she had been brought up and for her it was never questioned. Gran never for a single moment considered herself a foreigner though she had originally hailed from Ireland and had it not been the Irish that brought with them the gangs.

As we all sat in shocked silence Gran flew out of the room and all we could do was wait. She had one of those annoying clocks, the ticking of which seems to empathise the slowness of passing time. It accentuates the feeling of being interrogated a bit like the 'drip drip drip', the Chinese would use as a method of torture.

When Gran returned to her home she had a visitor with her. It was Jesus Christ's own employee in the form of Father Frank. Jackie was not the most devout of Catholics but she did have endearing respect for the priest who did a lot of good work for the children at the local chapel and community centre. Gran and all the family had known Father Frank for a long time. It was Father Frank who had given Gran first piece of the Body of Christ in the shape of a wafer when she made her Holy Communion.

Father Frank had been responsible for most of our family's events, the weddings, christenings, Communions, confirmations and deaths. He had been a great support to my gran through the years and Gran had been unswervingly loyal to him. She helped clean the church and saw to the flower arrangements. Father Frank, an Irishman who had come to Scotland in the 1930s, was at heart a good and holy man with the most endearing of temperament. He always saw the best in people and he never had a bad word to say about anyone.

'Jackie, my child - come here'; he said gently.

Jackie obediently did as the priest asked her to. Then, without warning, Father Frank slapped her face so hard that she lost her balance. As he walked towards the door he said in a voice that all could hear, 'may you burn in hell!'

With that the door slammed shut behind him and Father Frank was gone. I helped Jackie to up to her feet and we all just stood literally dumbfounded. Gran elbowed her way past us with a look of determination on her face and plainly she wasn't interested in Jackie or the baby. No, she was interested only in Father Frank and felt that he had administered both wisdom and justice in the vicious slap across Jackie's face. After his unexpected outcome Gran would never again see Father Frank at her house. Jackie, as could be imagined, was never welcome in gran's house ever again. Jackie for her part had no intention of returning and so it was going to be a battle of the wills.

The disgrace of an unmarried mother was too much to contemplate for most, even if it happened with disturbing frequency. An unmarried mother, made pregnant by a Muslim was too much for Gran to bear and from that moment on Jackie was a non-person. Was it an Act of God that the priest so heavily slapped her? What cannot be denied as afterwards the child was to be no more. Jackie didn't step foot in gran's house ever again and she never married. In truth, what we didn't know back then was that poor Jackie wouldn't live to a ripe old age at all. In fact she would never celebrate her fiftieth birthday.

Chapter 7
Glasgow's pearly Queens.

Jackie, unlike Gran, trusted her children and was determined to give them space. For this reason she didn't pay much attention to what was going on at the parties. Jackie had a consensual attitude towards drugs and she herself was no stranger to Marijuana. My aunt was fond of going clubbing with her mates at the weekends. After her weeks it was just what she needed. These occasions were opportunity to wind down and for a few hours at least be Jackie rather than mum. She had earned that much, she smiled. After all it was her life and she was already giving most of it away to her family and the chicken factory at which she worked eight hours a day.

Jackie and Maddie were of similar age and in fact were more like sisters than aunt and niece. My aunt's friend Mel had moved from Glasgow to London two years earlier. In between times they kept in touch and when Mel came to visit family they always hooked up. There was an occasion when Jackie took Maddie to London for a weekend. London beware, the pair had a riot.

At the time of their doing so Mel's friends had just come back from Amsterdam or the Dam as the Weegies (Glaswegians) called it. Her visitors didn't come back empty handed. That was not their way at all. They were loaded with hash and magic mushrooms that had been stored up their rectums. Any port in a storm was how one described the initiative.

Mel, Jackie's visitor or as some might say, accomplice, was a bit of a party girl. She had set her heart on ensuring that Jackie and Maddie would have a weekend they would never forget. As soon as they were suitably wasted the three girls decided to head to Blackheath Common with some supplies. A few of the guys had guitars and they all sat there in the sunshine enjoying a jam session. Chilling out to Fleetwood Mac and Neil Young, everyone was dreamily lost in a world of their own as they listened in to Harvest Moon and suchlike. Life was good and it was interesting.

No one was sure whose inspiration it was but later that evening they decided it would be a good idea to take an acid trip on top of the Ferris wheel. There you are then; you have ten Glaswegian nutters out of their heads taking acid on Blackheath Common. It was not going to be a knitting circle's outing was it? One of the guys freaked out and was doing the 'I see spiders routine.' They sent him home in a taxi but they never allowed such a hallucinatory experience as this dampens their lively spirits. Instead they headed for the nearest pub. Soon after, the arrivals, they were shown the door for being near hysterical, such was what Glaswegians would call simply good humour. The jolly band of virgins then headed back to Mel's and continued their lively night into the wee small hours.

By this time everyone was out of their heads and so this meant it was time for a bit of Pink Floyd. His Dark Side of the Moon was their favourite track of theirs. The music on this Floyd album has been described by some as unbelievable. At times it's strange and obscure, in some moments it's ethereal in beauty. At other times it is just plain rock and roll. It is a classic Pink Floyd track and will remain as such forever to be enjoyed by generations yet to come. Maddie says this album is Pink Floyd's gift to the world. Ah well, each, to their own. Through Alfie and Debs I was familiar with Pink Floyd albums.

Maddie, when younger was very anti-drugs but slowly and surely her opinion was changing. On a bit of a comedown from overdoing it far too much the revellers decided to carry on partying. The lively trio were putting mushroom tea down their necks on the double deck bus on the way back to Buchanan Street. Maddie says that when the 'shrooms' kicked in she thought she was on a space ship. The poor wee girl sat gripping the perfectly conventional bus seat like she was on a white knuckle ride at Alton Towers Theme Park. She truly believed that she was in a scene from Star Trek. My sister would later claim that this was the best experience she had ever encountered. She had really felt like she had been beamed up by Scotty and didn't she just love the experience! Afterwards she said that she sat on the bus totally still and completely comatose with a big silly grin on her face throughout the journey. Even after the passage of many years Maddie often talks about the mushies spiritual labyrinth and her orgasmic Star Trek experience.

Jackie was shortly afterwards to feel like Stig on her return and she would be completely depressed. My cousin Mickey threw a small party. This shindig was rapidly getting out of hand and surprise, surprise, it attracted the attention of the rozzers. If Mickey is to be believed everyone was having a great time chilling and dancing and the atmosphere was mellow. Not according to the neighbours and their families. They were deafened by the din of the music and the screaming off your head party. They had vented their frustration by calling the police to quell the disturbance.

During the police raid the officers confiscated Aunty Jackie's 'tomato' plants and later the dear was to receive a caution and a fine. This really got Jackie's goat and that was the end of the parties, from that moment on Maddie would have to find somewhere else to party. That was unlikely to pose much of a problem in Glasgow. It was about then that Maddie made the life changing announcement that she and Shona would be leaving Glasgow to go to London. I didn't believe their plans to be other than hot air and I for one didn't want them to leave me. But, they had made the decision and there would soon be new dramas to contend with. Trouble always followed that pair.

Having decided to up and head to London the idea was that they would get a job and they would share a flat. Until that arrangement could be fulfilled they would stay with my Aunt Bella whose home was situated in Camberwell in South East London. Things didn't go quite to plan. The pair had certainly not banked on facing a magistrate at Camberwell District Court within days of their arrival. It had been an unfortunate experience and maybe in other circumstances it was quite laughable. Whilst neither Maddie nor Shona were strangers to the magistrates courts they had never actually been on the wrong side of the law before.

After they had boarded the National Express coaches departing Glasgow's Buchanan Street and were headed for London's Victoria Bus station they decided to celebrate their new venture. The coach was as good a place as any to get into the swing of things and for sure, in their minds, they had plenty to celebrate.

Before boarding their bus they bought adequate supplies. This was not sandwiches, biscuits and bottled water but strong cider and Babycham. Without realising it, or perhaps it was in their fond belief that their entertainment and merriment would add value to the coach party's experience. Not quite. Their antics, which often bordered on hysteria, began to wind up the other passengers. After a torrent of abuse from one pissed off passenger Maddie and Shona called it a day and fell into a deep sleep whilst still almost upright in their coach seats. The travelling hours passed more peacefully for their fellow passengers but the excitement, if you can call it that was not quite at an end. Upon arriving in London they would then discover that their bags had been stolen.

They never had loads of cash to begin with and between them they had about £300. The sleepy two were now penniless. By the time they made their sad discovery the rest of the passengers had alighted and gone on their different ways. Maddie and Shona were paying a high price for their oversleeping.

Stuff happens and nothing could be done about it. They then decided to catch a taxi to Bella's house in Camberwell. No problem as it isn't too far from Victoria Bus Station. Putting their still bleary heads together they hatched a plan. It was decided that on their arrival they would do a runner and the cab driver could bear the loss. They were cunning enough to decide on an overweight driver and even looked out for one that smoked.

The 'ladies' found just what they were looking for or so they thought. He could be best described as looking like Giant Haystacks, the television wrestler. The fighter's girth was a national talking point. It got even better for this cab driver had a cigarette hanging from his fat lips. Their choice appeared to be tailor made for what the girls had in mind, for they could easily outrun that 'fat bastard.'

Fail! That fat bastard was as agile and as quick on his feet as an alley cat. It turned out that he could run like an Olympian on speed. With her mind in overdrive, Maddie, who knew Camberwell as well as a resident, told the 'fat bastard' where to pull in and to allow them to alight. By this time she had already advised Shona to run down a particular alley that led onto the main shopping parade. So Shona, who was clueless as to where she was supposed to be running alighted and legged it like he devil was after her. He was. She didn't get far. The next thing she knew the 'incredible hulk's' ham-sized fist was knotted in her hair and she was being hauled to account by the thoroughly pissed off taxi driver.

Dragging the deflated Shona into a newsagent he demanded that the shopkeeper call the police. Shona, still held in his vice-like grip, was twisting and turning in a vain effort to free herself. Maddie, seeing what had happened returned for Shona and that is how they found themselves tucked up in the back of the police car taking a one-way ride to Camberwell police station. Later, when Maddie would ask Shona what she had done with the dope they had brought with them from Glasgow, she confessed. She told Maddie she had panicked and of all places to discard it she had dropped it in the police car.

The taxi fare would have been a paltry ten quid. The hapless two were ordered to appear before the local magistrates the following Monday. There they would become again acquainted with the aggrieved cab driver, who just scowled in their direction. It could be assumed that he had better things to do with his time. This taxi driver's day was not about to get any better. The magistrate heard my sisters' account of how their bags had being stolen. They also told of how they had arrived in London from Glasgow and were looking for employment. He then took into consideration the rough manhandling Shona had received from the cab driver and they were each fined five pounds.

The driver aka known as Camberwell's Sumo wrestler was understandably incandescent at what he saw as an injustice. He was bawling his fat head off about the punishment not meeting the crime. The upset driver hotly exclaimed that this 'farce' was costing him money. He had to take the morning off work and all he had received in return was the fare and a small tip. That was one dude the girls hoped they would never see again and it was just as well they never did.

At least with that poor start behind them the two could move on and think to the future. Little did they know that it would only be a matter of time before the Gestapo would be on their trail and they would be returning to Glasgow earlier than they had anticipated; before that day they would have a little taste of London.

Aunt Bella was the oldest of my mother's sisters. A kind woman she was deeply religious. Her only regret in life was that she had never borne children. Married to a soldier serving in the Highland Light Infantry at eighteen Bella had married when she was eighteen. She would be widowed at a young age when his life would be taken in the line of duty. Bella had then decided a fresh start was needed and soon afterwards she secured a job as a nanny in London's affluent area of Mayfair.

The family who employed her didn't treat her very kindly. Bella felt with much justification that she was spending more time cleaning the family home than with the children. Deciding against accepting the role of drudge she saved every penny she could. Then, satisfied that she had something to fall back on, the unfortunate drudge handed in her resignation. After finding a small flat in Camberwell Bella landed a job in a local supermarket and there she settled into a much more settled and comfortable lifestyle.

Bella, the teenage widow, was in awe of London life. She was fascinated by its ambience and in particular its grand buildings. On Saturdays she would often wander around absorbing the atmosphere and she never got bored with the capital. There were however mixed loyalties as she never lost her Glasgow ties. I think it was through these infrequent home visits that my mother in Glasgow became more of a cockney than a Glaswegian. She delighted in the cockney phrases and quickly took them into her already rich vocabulary. On many occasions, when arguing with my father, she would say, 'Go on, and then fuck off with your Chinas.' I had no idea what she meant by 'Chinas' but later learnt it is Cockney colloquial for China plates as in mates.

My mother loved to theatrically throw into a debate, 'It's all gone horribly Pete Tong (wrong).' She would rarely miss an opportunity to throw in a bit of Cockney banter and as we grew up we added much of it to our own expressions. These would include 'use your loaf' and is commonly used in Glasgow. 'Stop telling porky pies'(lies). Most people are unaware that their everyday language is replete with slang that originated in London.

On hearing someone had died she would exclaim, 'Oh! I hear such and such is brown bread (dead).' It may well be that Bella's presence reminded my mother of her own little stint in London. She did have regrets of a sort and holding on to some of the Cockney banter relived the fond recollections she had of Britain's capital city.

When Bella visited Glasgow she invariably brought us children small treats. On many occasions I remember thinking that I wished Bella was my mum. It seemed so unfair that she couldn't have children when she would have been amazing as a mum. Sadly this was not meant to be. This was God's will and Bella just accepted her life as it was - she would never remarry. She toiled hard and had a good circle of friends through the church. Overall she was more contented with life than are many who have it all including a husband and kids. Again, be careful what you wish for. It must be supposed that many a married woman with children would kill to be single and independent.

To her credit Bella made Shona and Madeline very welcome at her home. She was genuinely glad of their company. Clearly it was going to be a bit of a squeeze but somehow the three would manage. There was work available and within a week of their arrival both Shona and Maddie had paid employment.

Madeline found employment working on one of the inexpensive ranges in a What Every Woman Wants store. This store retailed an inexpensive clothing range. Madeline wasn't happy with working Saturdays as, deprived of half a weekend; she would have to cut down on her party girl aspirations.

Shona, having spent a year in a secretarial college, had no difficulty in getting placed and was very soon to begin work in an office. Things were so different for the two adventurers in prosperous tourist-driven London than it was in Glasgow. Shona conceded that work opportunities had motivated them to make their move from the home city. One morning she had risen with the lark and over breakfast scanned the paper for junior office positions. There was a great demand for such and having secured a post she learnt that it was the first day it had been advertised. When Madeline had returned with a copy of the London Evening Standard, Shona couldn't believe how many jobs there were on offer. It got even better, for the salaries being offered were far higher than those offered in Glasgow.

Shona's first job took her to The Old Kent Road. This meant less time spent travelling and this was another bonus. Despite receiving more money than they needed to support themselves neither of the two was good at saving. There was no rush for them to do so, as Aunt Bella turned out to be pretty laid back. She just took a back seat and let them go about their business without comment or interference.

Shona had recently been thinking that she had left Glasgow under a cloud and wished their departure had been left on a better footing. Having left Scotland she wanted to put all that unpleasant commotion behind them. She had been 17-years of age when she left. When her father learnt of her intentions he went ballistic. Like an expectant father he was pacing up and down ranting and raving about making my sister a ward of court. In Scotland this can come into affect when a minor such as my sister was could be made a subject of a wardship order. This would mean Shona's ambitions to wander would be put on hold. Mother at the time of the upset was in the background and listening to my father spouting about his rights and the law. This she wryly found very much amusing. The jury must have been out when we realised that my father had been designated a pillar of the community. Mother then seemed unusually quiet but we put that down to it being her first beer. Only later on did we discover her true feelings. It was then the shit would really hit the proverbial fan.

Whatever, the outcome of his raving it was not quite

what we expected. We kids left the two of them to it. We were not all that fazed to learn that Maddie and Shona, regardless of his displeasure, were going to London anyway. No sooner had they made their plans but they were immediately off with their one-way tickets clutched in their hands. It was after the third tinnie had cascaded down Mother's throat that mum surprised us. 'Never mind him,' she said with obvious reference to me, Father who was looking like thunder said 'If that is your decision then you must go.' She shrugged as she dismissed my father's theatrical rage. She added simply that they must not make any of the mistakes she had made and to then be forced back to Glasgow as a consequence.

Mother was referring to the time when aged seventeen she had gone to London to live with her sister Bella. From what I gather she had a good time whilst she was there. It was the only time in her life that she would enjoy freedom away from my gran and her constant put downs. Mother soon after arriving in London had got a trainee manager's job as in a shoe shop and appears to have been successful. Mother took to London as a duck takes to water. She often told me that Londoners thought that the northerners had no sense of urgency. There was some truth in that. Laughing gently to herself, my mother would tell me that Londoners saw you as a foreigner if you came from north of Watford. Her stay in London unfortunately was short lived. She would have been at Bella's for about ten months when she received a letter. On opening it she found it was to say that my aunt Katie, who at that time would have been about sixteen, was pregnant. As a consequence there would shortly be a shotgun-wedding.

Chapter 8

Life in Glasgow

Mother's life would have been very much different had she not been obliged to return to Glasgow for the forced event. I think this was to embitter her throughout her life. Mother was consumed by thoughts of 'what if' had she either stayed or returned to the capital. She knew that by returning to her home city she had burnt her bridges. She never anticipated that her brief experience of liberation would be so compromised. Afterwards mother never again left Glasgow but set about taking life as it came with a very heavy heart.

Aunt Katie's wedding was a low key affair. It was bad enough for my Gran that her daughter was pregnant but it got worse. Katie's soon to be husband was a Protestant which often raised the anguished comment of 'what in the name of Jesus.'

Gran was aware of the bridegroom's family and in her opinion they were not of 'good Christian stock.' Rumour had it that his family where what was known as 'soup takers.' The term's origin could be found in the days of the Irish Potato Famine. It was back then that many Catholics converted to the Protestant faith in order to qualify for a free meal. Grandmother would often use me as her confidante as she said I was a good listener. I was far too well mannered to ever explain that this only appeared to be so. When she started to complain I would simply switch off and deep in thought I would nod at appropriate intervals. It was an arrangement that boded well for our relationship. Bleakly Mother told me that the day of the wedding was one of the most depressing days of her life and that no amount of praying would make right. Whilst telling me this she had this frighteningly transparent and almost vacant look in her eyes. Mother felt it in her heart that Katie was doomed to a life similar in prospects to her own. Her life would be eternally miserable and she would suffer extreme privation hard and this was hard for any mother to endure about her much loved daughter.

Grandmother was a cold lady and very solemn. What we didn't know was that Gran had lost her mother to mental health problems. She had taken her own life by hanging herself. Mother's mantle had been handed to Gran. It was down to her to bring up her brothers and sisters and it seemed that history certainly had a habit of reinventing itself. Gran would tell me that after leaving Ireland and coming to Scotland she never laid eyes on her siblings again. She somehow seemed relieved about this state of affairs. I presumed this was because the burden unloaded and the responsibility passed on. For sure Gran did not have a happy existence at all. As history seems to have a habit of recycling itself I often prayed for someone or something to break the vicious cycle which I blissfully thought it had to do at some point. Alcoholism and drug abuse was tediously and predictably transcending the family generations. It was like a curse but placed on our heads by whom?

Grandmother's life was about to change in a welcome way. This was sooner than she anticipated due to the fact that my father was to be jailed. Forthwith she would assume both the role of mum and dad. This would include getting us kids out of our beds and ready for school. She never questioned the unfair burden of it all. My mother had a severe case of lazyitus so was unprepared to take on the responsibility.

Gran worked in a hotel as a breakfast chef so was up with the birdies each morning and soon Shona was to be also. For six months Shona would be obliged to leave her friends and report to Gran every night. It was the same drill, to be in at 8 pm at the start of the Dallas theme music. My gran didn't know the meaning of the word flexibility so 8 pm meant 8 pm and a minute past was late.

A stickler for conformity she expected everyone to be thinking the same disciplined way. In truth she was so very appreciative of her Granddaughter's company. My sister Shona would be dropped off by taxi in the morning whilst Gran went on ahead to work. The job was in Glasgow's city centre and she had to be there for a six 'o'clock in the morning start. Shona was a latch-key kid and she had to sit in the cold until eight o'clock before she could get us up for school. She later told me that it was a task she would never consider repeating. I could hardly blame her.

On a few occasions, possibly through boredom, Shona would fall asleep in the chair. As a consequence we children would all overstay in our beds so there was nothing much new about that. It happened once too often and after a busted lip and a trip to the dentist to be treated for dislodged teeth Shona didn't sleep in again. Mother was out of her mind over Shona's transgression. She called her for all the names under the sun. Take your pick; they ranged from laziest bastard on earth to fucking halfwit. This was a not so endearing term that my mother enjoyed saying over and over again. Other epithets included fuck-face and the uncomplimentary charge that Shona was a fucking retard.

The expletives would usually come to an end with her

being called a retard. My mother had no concept that what was wrong was not Shona's fault but her own. Gran would later chastise her for her actions and mother found herself on the receiving end of a few equally rich curses.

Gran was to eventually retire from that job. This was because she was unfit to work after years of smoking tabs. She paid a heavy price and far more than what she had paid out in order to acquire her fixes. Her passage out of this world was through a gauntlet of ailments, respiratory diseases in the form of emphysema and cardiac and then finally through an oxygen tent. It is a pity that tombstones don't go into more detail as to why those who sleep in their little homes of clay got there before their time.

Before that unhappy exit she would allow herself to indulge in television. She was never more in her element than when engrossed in the television soaps. She would later watch her favourite programmes through a latex bubble. Her death was so upsetting that talkative Gran, of all people, would end up unable to speak without the aid of the oxygen mask. It was hard to imagine that this frail shadow of life had for so long ruled with an iron rod. Now on her deathbed she looked pathetic, frail and clearly a very frightened woman.

A battler to her end she would be missed greatly within the family when the time was ready for her passing on. Gran's way was to brush things under the carpet but as you get older and wiser you realise it was just her way of dealing with things. All this was just a facade for she had chosen not to reveal her true feelings. One was left to wonder about a gran whom we would never experience. It seemed that she held some unbearable secret. We could only imagine it by reading between the lines of her dear face. To show her feelings would have revealed her weaknesses and there could be no place for such sentiment in the only world we knew. It was a tough life in which only the brittle hard emerged at the other end relatively unscathed.

She had to be strong for the family. If only my mother and aunts had followed Gran's commandment: 'Keep your fucking knickers up and your knees together.'

Gran thought God was punishing her and she couldn't begin to understand why her own flesh and blood were causing her so much distress. Was her faith being tested? If so she was struggling, truly struggling. As for Katie's new husband, Gran loathed this man with a vengeance. She had made up her mind that he, a Protestant of all things, was the devil's spawn. He was exposed to be an infidel that had been programmed by the devil himself to penetrate her family. It was all she could do to bring herself to glare in his direction let alone a say a civil word in his presence.

Aunt Katie thought the arrival of the child and her married status would get her away from Gran and the aspiration did for a while. Little did she know that on many future occasions Gran would in fact support her and be there for her and her infidel of a husband. Aunt Katie, like so many others, would find out all too soon that the grass on the other side of the hill is not always greener.

Everyone in my family smoked. I remember Mother telling me that although she was two years older than Katie she was never allowed to smoke in front of my Gran. Thinking this was odd because at the age of eighteen you are classified as adult I asked why this was so. She replied simply, 'Katie is married.' Clearly marriage meant that law against smoking under age was null and void.

That was that! Marriage, regardless of age, carried a certain element of respect. This much was Gran rules and hey were irrevocable and equal to God's commandments and you without question abided by them. Mother was not to know that Katie's wedding would change her own life forever. Family and friends where invited over on the wedding evening. Although money was hard to come by the family all pitched in and helped. Some brought pretty much the usual suspects; there were the sausage rolls and sandwiches, cupcakes and suchlike. Others handed money over in the fond but futile hope that there doing so might better alleviate Gran's shame over the circumstances of her daughter's marriage.

Their intentions where good for they wanted to ensure an appropriate wedding reception. Aunt Katie had originally borrowed her friend's wedding dress. That was lighting the blue touch paper. When Gran saw that the dress she was to wear was white she totally freaked out. 'Holy Mary, Mother of God,' she screeched in her strong Irish accent. She then looked up to the heavens as though seeking divine intervention or inspiration. This was followed by a furious self-blessing ritual. One would have thought Lucifer himself had intruded on the occasion.

It was a momentous wedding celebration. She called Katie for all the whores, Jezebels and Mary Magdalene's she could muster. She then proceeded to hurl the dress into the fire's flames. I guessed there was a symbolism in this act of defiance. I am equally sure she thought she was acting on God's wish. It was unanimously decided that Katie would instead wear a dark blue suit for her wedding and that was the end of that.

It was around this time that Mother's fate would be sealed. She had known my father since they were children.

The pair had lived just a street or two apart in the strewn tenements of Glasgow's Maryhill district. These were not the most auspicious of surroundings. Maryhill at that time, to put it bluntly, was a rat infested slum in what was already a notorious dirty and industrial Glasgow. Its edifices were black from the soot of a landscape filled with countless acres of terraced homes and factories spewing fumes and smoke. As a child I recall father telling me that he thought the stone on the building was naturally black. Only years later would the city's buildings be cleaned. Then and only then did he realise that the stone was in fact much lighter. This cleansing period was a welcome and overdue breakthrough in the fight for better health that was introduced by the Clean Air Act of 1956. This initiative drastically reduced the environmental pollution that still caused so much respiratory illness in Glasgow and many other British cities like it.

The city of Glasgow was notorious for its grime, its violence, its underclass and cramped tenements. These hardships pressed down on the shoulders of a betrayed people who deserved much better. There was widespread overcrowding and the effects of extreme austerity imposed on the etched features of the people were self evident.

Our family's home was not untypical. It was cramped to say the least. Its three rooms provided what was ludicrously described as living space for two adults and ten children. One of these rooms was set aside for the girls. Floor space was at a premium as bunks and floor mattresses served their purpose and took up all the available space in the cramped quarters.

The two brothers had their own room, their being fewer in numbers there was for the lads more elbow room. Unsurprisingly there was incessant bickering. There wasn't even an inside toilet in this apartment though given the cramped situation inside our home the toilet's outside situation might be described as making the best of it. Tenement dwellers shared an outside toilet that could be found either on the landing or in the backyard. Money was in very much short supply and loo roll was considered a self indulgence too far. Those whose incomes did spread to toilet tissue were considered to be well off or posh. For the rest of us the newspapers served perhaps a better purpose than the one for which they had originally been intended.

To compensate for such hardships there was a strong sense of community. Folk pulled together. If a family was confronted by problems so immense that they threatened to overwhelm their already fragile existence the neighbours or family would step in to offer their support. There was in our downtrodden communities what might be described as an extended communal family. Anyone who failed in their obligation to clean a stairwell was soon on the receiving end of the community's wrath. Such matters as the cleaning of shared living space were dealt with on a rota basis.

There was a great spirit of camaraderie within these small and often isolated communities. Even here in the tenement there was a social class tier in which snobbery played its part. Such was the pecking order that keeping up with the Jones's was a social aspiration. Father often bragged that he was the very first person on the street to own a television. That was a class symbolism of social superiority.

To me I thought this surprising. I thought Daisy may have found this new technology to be too much of a distraction from their bible studies. She finally relented when her husband put foot his foot down. She thought it an unnecessary extravagance. Undeterred he; in forthright terms, pointed out to her that it was his money and spending it was his privilege. Father often explained to me that acquiring the television set caused him to become popular. As word of his acquisition got around the neighbourhood the family's new friends were appearing like cockroaches from the woodwork.

Television would make a big impact on father. For a start, Daisy was extremely prudent in allowing the children watch the set. She did relent and allow the siblings to watch the broadcast of the new Queen's coronation at Westminster Abbey. Unlike many Scots, Gran actually liked the English monarchy. She lapped up the pomp and circumstance, the grandeur and the splendour of the whole caboodle.

Before the arrival of television, people relied on the wireless (radio) for their information. The radio was never off in our household, especially during the course of the war. Radio was vital as a means of learning or keeping up with events outside one's community. The arrival of television was on a par with having a cinema in every household and when it was on the event would be marked by mother claiming her front row seat.

Mother would later tell me anecdotes and stories about the Rag and Bone man (bone-grubbers and rag-gatherers). These semi-itinerants, with their horse drawn carts, would collect unwanted household items and sell them on to merchants. These lower end tradesmen would trawl the streets collecting old rags, bones for making glue, and scrap iron as well as trading cheap items. There was little they couldn't find a use for. A child on hearing their approaching bell would offer contributions to the rag and bone man's daily harvest of unwanted items as the mites would often receive a balloon as payment or sorts.

White and coloured rags could fetch a couple of pence per pound weight and for this reason such offerings had to be dry. Coloured bones were considered of similar value and could be recycled to re-emerge as knife handles, toys and ornaments. When chemically treated the grease extracted from bones was useful for soap-making.

There were many times when my mother and her family would go hungry. After grandfather lost his leg to gangrene he became despondent and clinically depressed. For days at a time he wouldn't talk and everyone would tread carefully around him. It did not foresee a good day if one was to get on the wrong side of the old curmudgeon. He would often skulk off to the pub with his dole cheque and much later Gran would have to go and look for him. If she was lucky, and she was to quickly track him down he might have some of his money yet unspent by the time she located him. What she didn't know was that he had been running up a tab at his favourite pub and some weeks the dole money would be accounted for long before he even received it.

Gran for her trials and tribulations took in washing and she carried out sewing repairs. Her hard work was often fruitless. The money she earned from her toils would fall short of her and her family's needs. She simply couldn't give what she didn't have. As with so many other neighbours who found themselves in similar circumstances the local pawn shop was the Last Chance Saloon. The opportunity to place one's few belongings, jewellery, a man's suit; even a radio did help to make ends meet until things turned up. If the money credited in return was not returned then whatever had been left with the pawnbroker was forfeited. It wasn't unusual for Gran to call on her sons to pawn their suits on a Monday and recover them on a Friday so they could so they could set their dancing feet in the direction of the city centre's dance halls.

This was the norm and pretty much the lifestyle of our uncles each week. There would be no dance halls to attend during the weekend she needed the pawnshop's credit to buy food. Things were so desperate at times that children were sent scavenging with strict instructions bring back anything you can burn. As there was so much poverty in the area and when others were setting out to do the same thing they would often return empty-handed. Then, Gran had little choice but to start burning her own furniture. Ours was very much like other slum tenements. These were damp infested and freezing cold even in what passed for Scottish summers. At night the children would sleep huddled together with minimum blankets and coats covering them. Army coats were a favourite when tossed across the meagre blankets to help keep the chill. There were even occasions when blankets might be pawned.

When they were children mother and father were classmates. When father was a seven-year old he asked for my mother's hand in marriage. Be careful what you wish for. Little did he know then that his dream was to come true. The two remained inseparable through their lives. Mother on reaching her teenage years found herself in the family way and so the family could expect another shotgun arrangement very soon.

At this stage of her life Mother was a stranger to alcohol but was introduced to the devil's brew courtesy of my father. It was a Saturday night, not long after Katie's wedding, that Mother succumbed to his blandishments.

She and Father had been to the cinema and afterwards the pair had gone to a party at Katie's. Father by this time had secreted Eldorado Wine and a bottle of Olde English Cider in his bedroom. These same two bottles were also on their way to Katie's bash. Many years later, my mother when loose-lipped would confide in me that she couldn't abide taste of cider. She drank it anyway after which she discovered that having dropped her guard she had dropped her knickers too. On this happy or unhappy occasion my teenage soon to be mother was taken unceremoniously beneath a pile of coats in Katie's bedroom

And then there was Madeline and yet another shotgun wedding was looming. Gran was not having a very good time at all. Father was not too much of a disappointment to Gran, at least not after Katie's 'dancing with the devil' escapade. Grandmother had unwittingly low expectations of her daughters. It was enough for her that my father was Catholic and came from a very good Catholic background. During his childhood Father had been an altar boy at the local chapel. Gran albeit considered him to be a bit of a simpleton who was not cooking on full cylinders. To compensate he had one good thing going for him. He had a steady job with the council. Gran had known Father throughout many long years; she had after all attended his Christening.

I cannot recall a single occasion when she referred to him by his first name. Nor I cannot think that she ever did this to any of her son-in-laws. My Gran was good friends with my father's mother Daisy. She was the real deal paid up member of the God squad. A fanatical and devout Catholic she took her spiritual obligations to extremes. Sunday was a day for giving thanks to the Lord. She point blank refused to allow father or his brothers to play outside their home. Daisy was very much of the old school who believed children should be seen and not heard. The Victorian era had long since disappeared but it left Daisy and her principles behind.

Deeply loving of her brood Daisy felt it was her duty to God to make these children respectful. If that meant no frivolity on a Sunday then that was God's will. As a child, father knew well the Sunday regime. He would memorise the Rosary, submit to having his hair checked for nits, open his mouth for the obligatory syrup of figs to 'keep him regular.' There would then be Bible study followed by supper and bed.

Like my Gran, Daisy was not too happy about the impending betrothal. She made no secret that she blamed mother for 'this unfortunate situation' that they all found themselves in. It was to be dealt with in accordance to their beliefs and the Lord's will. After all, according to Daisy, that whore was stupid enough to drop her knickers!

She was not a big fan of my mother and through their married life that attitude was to never change. Yeah! These ladies had the brass neck to consider themselves as Christian, charitable, forgiving and Godly. You couldn't make them up.

When eight years old father was to discover that he had been an adopted child. Close to his mother, he was taken aback to learn that Daisy was not in fact his real mother. When he later discovered Mary to be his biological mum he was glad that Daisy had 'rescued' him. I think with attendance at mass and his being a choir boy, father without a doubt, during his younger years at least, was devoutly religious. As an adult he never attended church unless for a christening, wedding or event of similar importance. However I think he believed in Catholicism and he truly had faith that God was taking good care of him. He was not to know that later his faith would be sorely tested.

He didn't know either that his real mother and true siblings lived in the next tenement. He was painfully aware that Daisy had forbidden him from playing with the children there. Mary, who he knew as being Daisy's sister and therefore his aunt, were often perplexed. Why did they pass each other in the street yet refuse to acknowledge one another. There was never eye contact, nor a nod and most certainly never was a word exchanged. He couldn't possibly know that he was the cause of this strange family rift. At that young age he was unaware that Daisy on one fine day had marched into Mary's house. Immediately on entering she had lifted the sleeping infant from its cot, turned on her heel and left with the newborn child in her arms.

Daisy had often warned Mary that she shouldn't consider having more children as she couldn't cope with the brood she already had. In truth, Mary never had a choice when it came to family planning. Her husband did not know that no means no and neither Daisy nor Mary were under any illusions. All her children were born not from choice but through her husband's insatiable appetite for sex. It might be assumed that she was never made love to but was always taken on a mere whim. Mary knew better than to 'have a headache' and deny her husband. She had learnt that lesson the hard way and had no desire to having her ribs broken again. Even as she lay in agony he still took what in the eyes of God was his. She was his wife and in his perverted macho opinion he was entitled to his conjugal rights.

Daisy by taking the child from Mary believed that she carried out God's work. She had done so to save my father from those fornicating heathen. It didn't matter to her that Mary was her sister. There could be no acceptance of Mary's choice of lifestyle. Her sister had brought shame to her good family name. She was living with a scrounging lowlife; a lazy parasite and excuse of a man whose only concern was where his next bottle of cider came from and the ready availability of pussy.

Daisy had earlier discussed her concerns and intentions with the parish priest, Father Shamus. He had condoned her proposal and had given her his blessing for her to proceed with the 'abduction'. From that moment on father was in the hands of his aunt who would love him as only a mother should. He considered Daisy to be his true mother and as a good son he would love her dearly throughout her life.

On the other hand poor Mary did not have a good life at all. She had been used as a punch bag since she had once uttered those fateful words, 'I do.' Little did she know that with those two words her life was over before it had begun. Mary began to self medicate in order to block out psychical and physiological pain. It was a medication that came in the form of strong cider. The poor woman realised from early on in her marriage that she had pulled the short straw. By then the deed was done. She had made her bed and she was obliged to lie on it. It was only a matter of time before child number one arrived and things wouldn't get a whole heap better for her.

Her mother too, who was not sympathetic or supportive, had reminded her on many occasions that she had made her bed so now she could bloody well lie in it. Her end had been anything but godly. The God forsaken woman who had suffered so much through her life was to be found face down in a dirty puddle. This tragic discovery was made after she had been brutally raped and murdered leaving behind three motherless children. It was a scandalous story and even in a community much hardened to violence it was an ending that affected many. Not so Daisy, this unforgiving 'disciple of Christ' too the 'good riddance to bad rubbish' maxim to her uncharitable heart. The loss of her sister was of little consequence to her except perhaps as a relief. Daisy would go through the motions. Yes, she grieved and prayed or went through the motions but in her heart she was much relieved that there would be no risk of a claim on the boy she considered her son.

Father had never been permitted to talk to his 'real family'. It would be years later before he would be reunited with his 'biological family'. When my father later moved to the Glasgow's south side he was blissfully unaware that his real family was living a stone's throw away in the heart of Glasgow's Gorbals community.

Chapter 9
Giro Degradation

It was a miserable rainy day. My sister Deborah, whose lifestyle dreams had yet to be met, was living in a high rise in Glasgow's Gorbals district. Most days were tedious regardless of whether it rained or not and all, were predictably routine. However, on this fortuitous day she would by chance literally bump into a stranger in a local bar. As the two collided the upset drink cascaded down her front. Deborah was none too amused. She quickly grasped a bar towel in a vain attempt to right the wrong the stranger had inflicted upon her. She did so as her unwanted acquaintance tried in vain to make amends for his awkwardness and for which he unreservedly took full responsibility. His attempts to mop up the spilled Pernod and blackcurrant drink were done to a glowering backdrop of feminine indignation. If this dude didn't stop apologising whilst wiping her down he would be decked she thought to herself. Red-faced with embarrassment and the unwanted attention they were attracting the guy offered to buy her a replacement drink. The dour expression on Deborah's face suggested to him that this was trivial compensation. He then took matters a stage further by pressing a fiver into her hand.

'This will cover the cleaning bill,' he smiled.

Less livid she accepted the offer of a drink and grabbed the fiver for the cleaners whom it must be said would never see Deborah walking through their doors with the soiled garment to be cleaned. The top wasn't worth it and would likely be binned.

Deborah's purpose in going to the bar was a much looked forward to game of pool with Maddie and

Shona. Over their pool game they would exchange pleasantries and banter with other locals. One of the lads in the small throng was a cocky little asshole. He was notoriously mouthy and on this day he was firing on all cylinders. In other words he was giving it 'the large un.' This was Glasgow speak for trying to impress the ladies with his perceived tough guy status and connections to the rival Maryhill district. This strategy was perhaps due to Maddie having mentioned that she knew quite a few people who lived in Maryhill. There was a little name swapping going on.

You know how it goes: 'Do you know wee Jimmy?' In Glasgow there is a high probability that you will know someone whose sobriquet is 'Wee Jimmy.'

The lads were roundly beaten by the lassies. All of these champions were in the ladies pool club and pretty well rated. Having routed the lads the group retired to a bar table where they could engage their minds and tongues. It was then that things got interesting. Included in the group were four guys who were all living in the Gorbals high rises. Two of them were brothers whose family originally came from Maryhill.

Maddie had remarked that most of those she knew where too old for them to remember her parents. My father and mother grew up in Maryhill but they had not been frequent visitors since moving to Glasgow's south side. Furthermore, my family were not exactly notorious and there was only a slim chance that my Uncle Charlie might have been known through acquaintances.

One of the group that day was Mark. For some yet unknown reason at the time he was known locally as Stanley. The girls found him to be highly amusing and were quite intrigued by the name change. Mark, or Stanley, told them a few years younger he had been a bit of a lad and got into a spot of bother. This was taken to mean gang rivalry. Gangs were commonplace in Glasgow, especially in the Gorbals. The community's notoriety was well founded. It certainly produced more lowlife shit than any other municipality of its size. Stanley recollected a while and he then explained to the girls around the table that at one time things got really heavy. In fact they got so heavy that he was obliged to carry the more modern equivalent of a cutthroat razor. This was the handyman's tool known as the razor-sharp Stanley knife, hence the name Stanley. Only then did the name change make sense.

The credibility of his story went unchallenged. Shona would tell me that by the look of the scar. Such blemishes are in local slang known as a Mars Bar. Stanley had been on the receiving end of much cut and thrust and had given as good as he had taken.

Appearances have a lot to do with how you perceive people. This guy sounded intimidating but he was said to be nice. He had it seemed 'squared himself up' and put all that shite behind him. Looking forward to a more conventional future he was now re-training on a Youth Training Scheme.

The Youth Training Schemes had been on the receiving end of much political criticism, a negative press and local scepticism from their well intentioned start. The idea was you that you spent nine months on a selected job training occupation in conjunction with three months at a college or higher education institute. The scheme was not optional. You didn't have a choice but to enrol in such a scheme: if you were a school leaver between the ages of 16-17 and were unemployed. For your efforts you received a miserly £30 each week and this was your lot until you reached eighteen-years of age. It was seen as a form of governmental enforced labour but in theory, as are all things, it was a good well intentioned idea. In practice the scheme was shamefully abused by employers who used it as a source of cheap labour. Who knows, maybe Stanley had a future after all.

One thing I will say about Glaswegians is that they are very much what you see is what you get. They are candid and often self-deprecating. You could be stood at a bus stop and within minutes you will learn the life history of the stranger you were stood next to. The sentiment such conversations carry is a genuine sincerity and you can meet the most interesting people as a consequence of this trait.

At the inn that day, where the snooker had been played, the second conversationalist was a little on the loud side. This garrulousness was, in all likelihood, fuelled by multiple beers but he was hardly alone in that failing. It was learnt that this guy had moved to Glasgow from his hometown of Aberdeen and so was now known as Angus. He had lived in this area for just the year. We learnt that he had family back home. When as a worker on the oil rigs he received his redundancy notice his move to Glasgow seemed an obvious solution to his redundancy. There in Scotland's capital city could be found reasonable rents and work opportunities. There was only one problem with the intention. In Glasgow there wasn't much call for riggers who were experienced in oil rig work. Unsurprisingly his dreams had evaporated and he was now back on the old King Cole otherwise known as the dole.

The ever resourceful Angus supplemented his meagre income with a little ducking and diving. Weed on that day was being passed from hand to hand and there were pills involved too. Nothing too heavy and, of an anti-social nature; rather than their being on a truly criminal level, this extra activity funded Angus's social life such as it was. Deborah decided against incivility and cash and weed then changed hands once again. At this pointed the group decided that they would return to Deborah's place and continue their socialising there.

Picking up their carry-outs from the bar the small group trooped out of the bar heavily focused on the shindig they had in mind. Once they group had arrived at Deborah's home they chilled. In the background could be heard the dulcet tones of Tom Waite. As anticipated the drugs were dished out among all present and incorrect.

In that group that day was Justin and Joey. Twin brothers, they had been born and raised in the Gorbals but they came across as the more streetwise. Both of the brothers worked which in itself was unusual. They seemed pleasant enough characters and appeared to be self-confident and comfortable in their skins.

It turned out that the pair had connections to Maryhill and that was how on the first occasion the girls met their biological cousins. When Maddie mentioned the street my parents grew up in there was a spark of recognition gleaming in the twin's eyes. The name had a familiarity for it was where they claimed their father had come from. The penny finally dropped for Shona when it was mentioned their grandmother Mary and in the same breath Aunty Daisy.

After tossing a few family names around it transpired that their father and our father were brothers. Any lingering doubt was dispelled by their explaining the tragic tale of Mary. What a small world indeed.

At this revelation there was a heady mix of

consternation, surprise and happiness. Strangers had become family and close family, not even extended relatives, but close family members and all by chance now sitting around the same table. This would be the start of many a rendezvous with our new cousins. After the lads went home Maddie and Shona sofa-surfed but before retiring to night's sweet bliss the two shared their nostalgic moments. High in their considerations was to wonder what my father would make of their chance discovery. A mental note was filed that sleepless night. Maddie decided Father would be told of the exciting discovery the following morning. How thrilled he would be, Maddie thought quietly to herself, of that she could be assured. The anticipatory smile was still on her delightfully sweet face as she then slept the night away.

That was not quite how things turned out. For a dismal start it was the afternoon when she awoke. The sun had in fact long passed its zenith and was now sinking ever faster to the unseen horizon. After the previous day's partying the three girls were all hung-over and their dehydration spoke volumes. It was then unanimously agreed that a hair of the dog was what was thought to be the best solution to their lack of sparkle. As might be expected a few others were to soon join the small party. Surprise! Surprise! A bit of a session took place and when Maddie, Deborah and Shona turned up at Mother's home they were by that time half-cut to say the least.

The greeting was hardly open armed. You get the feeling you are unwelcome when your host greets you with, 'What the fuck do you think you lot are fucking playing at, turning up rat-assed at this bastardly hour.'

You could say Mother was as browned off as any Trinidadian. Mother's sanctimonious abuse continued until her glaring eyes softened at the sight of the bags of tinnies. It was a timely peace offering if you like and welcomed in the manner intended. This was the only time I ever saw my sisters drinking with Mother and without drama. It soon got a bit too much for Shona and not long afterwards she staggered off to her bed. The next lightweight would be Maddie and so it was finally left to Deborah to tell the tale of their family reunion of a kind. Mother took it all in and as she listened to her daughter there was a thoughtful expression on her face as Deborah told her of their happy event.

'Don't tell him.'

In disbelief Deborah shook her head from side to side as if to say, 'Am I hearing you properly?'

There was nothing wrong with my sister's hearing. What we couldn't understand was the lack of logic behind her father's unexpected response. The news was something she had a right to know but she had a different take on the unexpected reunion. Mother explained that Father, the twin's uncle, would not be interested and added that things would be best left unsaid. Debs never let it be known that her thoughts never harmonised with her mother's. She decided, 'fuck it,' She was going to tell him anyway. What harm could there be in stating the bleeding' obvious. After all, she wasn't in the habit of taking too much notice of her mother. She thought to herself, 'why the fuck should I take a blind bit of notice of her now?'

Deciding to track father down there was little need for the skills of legendary tracker Eddie McGee or even Sherlock Holmes. When looking for father you need look no further than his usual watering hole. Father loved to sing ballads and he stored his guitar behind the bar. The choice of music was invariably country of the cowboy kind. There was occasional tributes paid to the Beatles but mostly it was get your Stetsons on your head time. The pub's landlady, Fiona, was good natured and happy to go along with it. Her regulars lapped it all up. That was always the case until Father got a bit too pissed and his soothing warbling descended to slurred dirges. 'Hey, Debs!' he calls as their eyes met.

Deborah smiled indulgently, her dear heart racing in anticipation of revealing her glad tidings. Furthermore, it must be added that the drinks she ordered just couldn't come fast enough for her. Without undue delay she blurts out the news of their by chance meeting her father's twin brothers. She was delighted at making this weekend one of the most memorably in her fond dad's life. She did that alright but she did so for the wrong reasons. She really and truly should have listened to mother. In truth and in her favour it must be said that my sister wasn't too sure what to expect after the little chat with Mother.

Father scowled. 'Hey, Deborah! Keep away from them lot. They really are bad bastards. They are basket cases so don't be seen dealing with these dudes.'

Debs was now totally confused. Surely the importance of the disclosures last night couldn't be lost on him as he had never even met them. Surely there must be some mix up and he was probably confusing them with someone else's progeny. When all was said and done the three sisters had spent all night with Joey and Justin and they were clearly good eggs.

As it turned out Father had known for years that his brother had moved to the Gorbals and he was also painfully well aware that his brother had two sons. Unbeknown to Deborah, years earlier her father had a chance meeting in a city centre bar and the two brothers recognised each other from childhood. As my father had been adopted by my grandmother the two men who had met that day by chance had different surnames so there had been no association. My father then told Deborah that his brother Dougie was employed by a loan shark company and his two sons, his nephews, were his lackey's enforcers. They had no qualms about the dirty side of their grey area business. If an evil deed was to be carried out then so be it. What is a broken knee cap between friends? Those who were terrorised and victimised tended to get the message. If that methodology didn't sink in there were ways to encourage compliance to agreements. Some might describe it as torture, as last resort which usually worked well.

The interest rates on the shark loans were already sky high. They were unaffordable but this was not known to those uneducated unfortunates who couldn't grasp interest rates. Worse, if any debtors fell behind on payment the interest would be doubled. When you are in a hole you stop digging but there were too many hapless creditors who kept on digging, in some cases their own graves. Loan shark business in such boroughs as Maryhill and the Gorbals was brisk. The council had made tentative social progress and some good work had come about but a lot of the high-rise apartments were unsuitable for the poor families they housed. The predatory and callous nature of loan sharks that were thriving in such a pool of derelicts operated in a vacuum and was beholden only to themselves. Few if any questions were asked when a loan was requested. What was the point? Few applicants had a credit history worth looking at and fewer had collateral. There was only one form of repayment guarantee, not the courts but enforcement.

Loan sharks proliferated on a territorial basis and such was heir thuggery that they were not the breed you grass to the cops. To do that would mean unbearable victimisation and undeniably violence. Doing a runner through self exile wasn't an option unless the family vacated their home. What then, homelessness? The enforcers knew they were all-powerful. The interest rates on the loans were of course daylight robbery and in a very thin veneer of legality. Loan sharks were 'providing a service' but the price was more than fiscal. Their currency was terror through enforcement.

The sharks had a captive market for the Maryhill and Gorbals communities were stuffed with abandoned single mothers who each and every day struggled to make ends meet. Some tenement blocks were better than others but many had elevators. These lifts stank of piss that was so bad you wished you had worn a gas mask when visiting. Occasionally some scumbag would shit and for a laugh smear excrement on the lift buttons for good measure.

Most of the tenement tenants were unemployed and probably unemployable. Their address alone was enough to discourage any potential employers. Such unfortunate people were totally dependent upon social security, their sick and unemployment payments.

Single people would regularly receive a Giro cheque. In order to qualify for state handouts they were obliged to sign on at the dole office every two weeks. It worked differently if you were single and had dependants. Single mothers were not required to sign on fortnightly and instead they were issued with a cheque book. The meagre amount could be cashed each week at the post office. Everyone knew what the 'Monday book' was. That was the day when one could expect to find long queues of dependents at the communities' post offices. Faced with constant shortages and high prices it was not unusual for some desperate mothers to fall behind on their loan repayments. If they reneged on obligations due to the loan sharks their Giro books would be confiscated by a suited thug and used as security for the loan. On the following Monday these wretched creditors would be escorted to the post office by the company's enforcers. When the poor unfortunate borrower cashed their cheque the lowlife took what was owed. These mounts were excruciatingly inflated.

There were occasion when a luckless borrower owed more money to the sharks than the state handout money they collected. When that occurred the book would be confiscated until the following Monday. There was no sympathy afforded towards those distressed. There was never a thought given to the bairns left behind at the distressed mother's home. That was not the loan sharks concern; this was the punter's problem. It was held that the borrowers knew the rules when they applied for the loan. Deprived of the only source of loaned income they had the vicious cycle was self perpetuating. As Eli Khamariov observed; 'Poverty is a punishment for a crime you didn't commit.'

Near to the flats there were several small shops. Usually one of these would be the fish and chips shop known as 'the chippie.' Of course the community's jetsam and flotsam would congregate in its vicinity. There would be a newsagent, an arcade, maybe a chemist or betting shop. The locals would squander their Johnny Cash on the arcade's fruit machines. The grandly named shopping malls and parades would be the community's social centre of sorts. Many of the locals were those living on the fringes of civilised society. These would include the smack-heads, the glue snifters, some of whom were known to Deborah.

Such places were not well policed and they are very intimidating, especially at night. The chippie was open for business until midnight. It was the perfect place to go to if you needed cigarettes or skins (Rizla cigarette papers). Such shopping locations would not be complete without an Off-Licence shop where alcohol products were sold. There was a half decent kebab and pizza takeaway and, without a sense of irony, often its name would be associated with some exotic paradise such as Tropical Sunset or Marbella Beach. You might also expect to find in such malls and parades a 'Ruby Murray'. This was a curry based takeaway. There would be no orders taken and handed over unless you paid up front. The shop owners were wise, far too many of them had taken their completed order and legged it out of the shop.

There was a flower shop and a bicycle shop. Both closed down as they were no longer able to meet the cost of their retail insurance premiums. One of these retailers had been robbed over twenty times before the owners decided to call it a day. Other than that there was the Post Office and that was more or less it. Anything else was boarded up and likely covered in graffiti.

On Mondays, Deborah would avoid the parade like the plague. By 9am, before the Post Office's doors opened, a queue would have formed outside. One often heard the wailing and sobbing as a distraught mother would plead, 'Don't take my book, what about my bairns?'

Shona said it was a pitiful sight to see. I am sure it was unbearable. Some dependent on state handouts, through no fault of their own but because of errant fathers, were anxious and in distress. It was not unknown for some distraught mums to offer their tormentors blow jobs even if their inducements were a public spectacle. Such problem beset women had sunk to levels that left them without hope, pride or shame.

What was going on was common knowledge but people knew it best not to interfere. If you were prudent you turned and looked the other way for really that was the only option. You never knew who you would be dealing with. There was no shortage of rotten eggs that were far lower down the morality scales than were their ill-fated victims. Little mercy could be expected. In this part of the city it was wise to observe the three wise monkey practice of see no evil, hear no evil, speak no evil.

There were a lot of drug dependents in the Gorbals and no shortage of alcoholics. The Council, in its infinite wisdom, decided it would be a good idea to coral problem tenants under one semi-isolated reservation. Many people, who had been born and raised in the Gorbals, didn't fully appreciate that this wasn't a solution. The Council, charged with housing its population, did its duty. Having met their commitments the problems caused became the responsibility of other departments. It was social engineering filed under the heading, 'pass the buck.'

The locals were far from being compliant. Where Deborah's flat was situated she was lucky that there were at least working CCTV cameras. There was also a concierge and an absence of the acrid stench of stale urine. Nevertheless, even reflecting on visits to her, leaves a sour taste on one's mouth. There was an old type tavern opposite the flats and that is where many locals could be found. It isn't often you find junkies in pubs. No one wants to see them in bars for even the most wretched of people feel nothing but contempt for drug addicts. As far as many ordinary people were concerned, addicts were beyond redemption. These really were the dregs and looked upon like they were something the cat dragged in. Whilst that was what people might have inwardly thought, when the Jaggers came round the bars selling their stolen wares, they would sing a different tune. Then, during the few moments it took to exchange stolen goods for dole money they were best of buddies.

Glasgow pubs had a reputation for black market transactions. There wasn't much you couldn't buy or order when your face was a familiar sight. It is much more tightly controlled now but it was once commonplace for butchers to call in on a Saturday afternoon. They would bring with them a few bags of meat that they would sell for half price. When the junkies cottoned on to how much cash they could make selling meat they just tanned the butchers and sold the meat for a pittance. What has to be remembered is that junkies become so desperate for a fix that they would happily sell their own mothers to get what they want. If you could catch a junkie 'rattling', a turn of phrase meaning desperate for a fix, you didn't need powers of persuasion or negotiating skills to get what you wanted in return. You had them over a barrel and they would take what they could get.

The junkies were thought of as pond life. Even the underclass felt superior to the junkie class. Society spurned these ailing people and their lives were considered utterly worthless. When people recognise you for what you are, a shameless thieving junkie, then empathy and sympathy are in short supply. Those words came from Alfie. When his drug-fuelled paranoia was at its most extreme Alfie didn't venture out so often. Occasionally, when accompanied by

Maddie, he visited Debs when she had her flat. The truth is he was not very much welcome. My sister did not want him to visit regularly as, at the time, Alfie would jack you up and steal your socks if he could. Deborah never did have much of value but what she did have she valued; if you get my meaning. The last thing she needed was Alfie stealing the little she had. She couldn't take her eyes off him. When Alfie was younger and bolder he would take his swag to the Gorbals. There were always buying punters and he rarely came back empty handed.

Chapter 10
The Terrible Twins

Alfie had been in the same bar that Shona was drinking in the night she met the twin brothers. Quite shocked by these latest revelations about her cousins she decided to ask Deborah to put the word about and find out what she could. They wouldn't have to wait very long for the dirt to be dished up. Deborah and Shona having arranged to meet at the bar was only just though the door when they bumped into Stanley. He had remembered that they were related to the twins and it was natural for them to ask after them. This never aroused any suspicion on Stanley's part. The two schemers plied Stanley with shots and it wasn't long before his lips were looser than a hooker's pussy.

Apparently, the two being enquired about were fast-footed quick-thinking little entrepreneurs. Having said that they were not quite the level to find themselves on Dragon's Den. This was the television programme for the more conventional types of up and coming business executives. Nonetheless they had their fingers in a few pies and were impressive in their ability to rake the money in. Their most recent inspired enterprise was to extort money from prostitutes. That wasn't too difficult as often the girls would approach them. As Stanley (Knife) put it, it was a case of mutual agreement. The two brothers offered the girls protection without the heavies being present. Many thugs preyed on girls in the so-called sex industry but people knew that if they were under the protection of the two Js they would leave well alone. It was money for old rope really.

There were plenty of girls, mostly but not necessarily drug addicts who were happy to turn a trick in their apartment for what was described as easy money. In the Gorbals the girls were safe in the knowledge that they had paid for protection. However, off their home turf it was no way José, and if they worked away from home they were on their own.

What with the twins' loan sharking and making money from the ladies of the night it is a wonder the boys had any time for parties. Father had been spot on in his description and he was so right with his warnings for us to keep away. Whatever, the girls genuinely liked the two brothers so as usual no heed was taken. Father knew that his nephews had a rough reputation and his own brother was not going to get sainthood any time soon. Word did get around the grape vine that father had no wish to be associated with the twins. Few however knew of the blood relationship, which pleased him. If things get nasty then rival thugs will often target a rival's family members. Father was prudent in keeping his daughters out of another kind of dragon's den.

There were yet to come a few parties at Deborah's. This was a good period for her as she was trying to reduce her medication. This meant she had sufficient energy to at least go to the pub for a game of pool. Those were times of contentment for Deborah.

We had a sort of family get together for Maddie's birthday and several regulars from the Tavern called in. This was the first occasion that I would be introduced to my roguish cousins. At first I was quite wary as I had heard all the stories. Clearly they were evil fuckers and I was under no illusions. I thought the least I could do was offer them an olive branch and then judge for myself if they should be given the benefit of the doubt.

Shona and I, are an intuitive pair and we tend to rely on our femme intuition about people. My instincts were screaming that these two were as bad as it gets. The pair had a cocky swagger about them and strutted like they were the dog's bollocks. They knew of course that their reputation went before them. Justin and Joey were well aware of the threat they posed and it might be supposed the 'respect' they thought theirs as a right.

In their presence at that party I felt on edge throughout the occasion. There was in there a definite tense atmosphere. When your almost primitive survival instincts surface, you know it is about to erupt. Well, not too long into the party the lava was flowing in the form of claret and no way was it the bottled kind of nectar. There had been some sort of silly row going on in the kitchen. From it we could hear swearing and accusations being levelled about someone nicking beer. Such pilfering is very much frowned up by Glaswegians. To be light-fingered at a hosted party is to commit a cardinal sin and wars have been waged for lesser sins.

It all happened in a flash. One minute there was raised voices and that in itself is no big deal in a party atmosphere. However, this was abruptly followed by howls and screams that were followed immediately by an eerie silence. Someone had had their throat sliced open. My first thought was that Stanley had lost the plot but the finger of accusation could not be pointed at him. He was comatose and stretched out on the sofa and he was well out of the action. The rest of us were clueless as to how to handle this totally unexpected and definitely unwanted incident. Someone quick wittedly grabbed a towel and tried to compress the victim who was haemorrhaging blood. They were doing this while the twins were getting the victim out on to the landing and roughly shoving him into the lift. It was then that, having got the injured man into the elevator they pressed the ground floor button and stepped back as the doors closed.

What was all that about Maddie asked a visibly shaken Shona? Deborah piped up, 'Your clever cousins got rid of the evidence so there would be no cops on the scene.'

Debs knew who the slasher was but she didn't know from Adam the identity of the unfortunate bastard who would need more than throat soothing pastilles. Maddie and I cleaned up the blood and after a few moments the party just carried on as if nothing had happened. Debs in her own way was glad the brothers had so coolly and competently dealt with the matter.

She later learnt from the bragging concierge that he, the caretaker of the tenement was now a local hero. Wasn't he the one who had saved this guy's life? Having heard the commotion he checked out the CCTV cameras. Spotting the victim he had promptly dialled the emergency services. Apparently the victim kept his mouth shut and fortunately he survived. The police placed posters in the vicinity stating that there had been a vicious attack. The cops suggested that anyone with information should come forward. Anonymity was assured but there were no takers for no one was ever going to risk being exposed as a grass. The matter from there on was a dead duck. I often wonder if the slashing incident might have been somehow connected to Debs being gang raped. Had it been pay back time. Of course I shall never know.

Maddie is one of those people that have extraordinary recollection. She swears blind that she can remember things from when she was about five months old. We often joked that she could remember the umbilical cord being cut. Yet this is the same Maddie remember, who had difficulty in going to the shops and remembering what she had gone for. Sometimes, when she had these bouts of wistfulness she would 'remember' things that simply didn't happen. She loved to tell people that her hair was once so long that she could sit on it. This was not true at all, it was sheer fantasy. As we children all became older we learnt the art of diplomacy and we would not embarrass her. We would simply nod and amiably agree. I am glad for Maddie that her brain has the capacity to distort the truth!

Our Mandy was my Aunt Katie's youngest daughter and this whippet had a truly vicious streak in her. On many occasions Maddie would be on the receiving end of Mandy's spiteful little ripostes and Maddie would fatefully become Mandy's punch bag. Although of similar age they were not of a similar nature. My aunt Katie was often pulled up to attend the school about her daughter's disruptive behaviour. From a very early age we had a suspicion that 'something about her was just not right.' She had been diagnosed with social and dysfunctional behavioural problems. The girl enjoyed being the class clown and delighted in doing things behind the teacher's back. Her misdemeanours included giving him the Vicky (two fingers up) and cheeking him back.

Sure the other kids laughed but they were laughing at her and not with her. It was a cry for attention and it didn't go unnoticed. Father had an air rifle that used slugs shaped like bullets. It looked the business and it was weighty and looked like a real rifle. When standing at the open window he would let us have a shot at the tin cans placed neatly on the wall of our communal yard. Whilst everyone was taking aim Mandy would purposely aim for the stray cats. It was unusual behaviour for a child to display, especially a girl. Mandy just wasn't wired up properly.

These days, with more modern psychoanalysis, she would be identified as potential psychological loose cannon. It wouldn't be too long before Aunt Katie would have a visit from the social services. Apparently Mandy had a school attendance problem and letters demanding explanation from the school weren't being answered. Katie was at the time working in a local bar and was not at home during the day so was unaware that her daughter was skiving.

Neither Katie nor Mandy were fazed. For heaven's sake, what was the big deal? Her daughter was only killing time by ticking attendance boxes. Anyway, she would be leaving school in a few months time. Katie, the ever devoted mum told her unwanted visitors to fuck off and stop wasting her fucking time. Then, on arriving home she clipped Mandy round the chops and blithely began to prepare the dinner. Most nights the two had cheesy mac and never seemed to get fed up or complain about the tedious predictable burnt offering. I supposed they had not much to make comparisons with and in a way they were like cattle, happy with their lot and never questioning their position in life. In the summer it was grass, in the winter it was hay. They were just used to bland. Not only were the evening meals repetitious for their breakfast was invariably porridge.

Katie couldn't be bothering with cooking, especially after she had been on her feet all day. After her day at work was completed she had important things to do and to think about. Uppermost in her mind would be where she could get some money from to purchase beer. In all the coming and going between social services and our family the jobs worth, highly paid, never served any purpose or achieved anything at all. All the palaver was a complete and utter waste of tax payer's money. They were vacuous box-tickers. My mother remarked that they should be lined up and shot but we thought that a bit extreme.

Mandy returned from the shops one fine day and my aunt Katie asked her if she had been smoking. Katie denied all knowledge of her doing so but she knew she was caught bang to rights. The wretched youngster stunk of nicotine and smoke. Katie lunged at her daughter but Mandy deftly sidestepped. Not before her mother grabbed a fistful of jumper. As Mandy retreated she was forced to release her hold. That was when it happened. The cigarette ends, the evidence commonly known as douts, cascaded to the floor.

Mandy had started smoking, it got worse, much worse; she had actually been collecting discarded cigarette butt ends from the streets. When discussing the situation with Mother Aunt Katie told her that she had told Mandy that the butts were full of piss. She then proceeded to push the discarded cigarette butts down her daughter's protesting throat. It was a harsh lesson but obviously didn't get through as Mandy by then was just another Nicotine Lil. When she was a little older Mandy would hang out with Maddie. As time was the great healer they were by this time no longer each other's Nemesis. The relationship was sort of a meeting of minds and hearts. Maddie didn't really take to her cousin. Strangely, she said that she felt sorry for her because she was such a lying prat. I couldn't understand the logic in that statement.

It was however true for Mandy was a serial liar. She would lie just about everything even when it was unnecessary for her to do so. She would tell the kids at her school that she was Simon le Bon's niece. She hoped that by name dropping the name of the lead singer of the boy band, Duran Duran the kids would be in awe of her. It didn't matter that it was complete bullshit. She thrived on the attention her lies brought to her. She once told friends that she had a new puppy and they were welcome to call in and make friends with it whenever they were passing. Mandy was mortified when later that day two children turned up and were desperate to see the puppy. The hapless liar had to think fast. She told her unexpected visitors that the puppy dog had died and her mother had buried it. There was of course no puppy and there was no reason for her lie. Her doing so, simply revealed a very insecure child trying desperately to make friends and to better fit in. I assume that is why Mandy liked Maddie. She instinctively knew that her companion had gone through all that shit herself. She was trying to fit in and it just didn't happen for Maddie. It wasn't happening for Mandy either.

The problem with being a liar is your having to have a good memory. The alternative is to keep the lie as close to the truth as possible. Mandy never had the intelligence to remember this truism. It wasn't long before she would have the new moniker and was better known as Betty Bullshitter. Gran had a saying that she would often spout. 'Tell that to the Marines." No one really understood the expression's origins. I did. As so often in Britain it had its genesis in the sea. The term comes from 19th Century Royal Navy. Sailors were usually more experienced in seamanship than were the Royal Marines, which was more of a light infantry skirmish party. When a far-fetched tale would come up in conversation; the term: 'tell it to the Marines' was used, as it was said that the Marines were naive enough to swallow anything.

Poor Mandy was not having a good time of things at all. She was slightly more aloof than nonchalant; she was quite a private person and was not particularly interesting. Because of her penchant for fantasising few would tolerate Mandy being in their company. This meant that poor Mandy was so in some ways, like Maddie, a maverick and a loner.

Aunt Katie was too blind drunk and uncaring to understand that Mandy would have future mental health issues. Her older sister Trina had long since been hooked on heroin but that wasn't the direction that Mandy was heading. Sure she dabbled. Everyone dabbled in drugs but it was no big deal as most users know their limits. Mandy never got involved in the drug scene but she liked an occasional reefer. Unfortunately it made her paranoid as it does most users. Having watched Alfie when he was suffering that condition she made a choice not to become too deeply involved and she had the commonsense to keep well away from the bongs.

Mandy wasn't the partying type at all and was uncomfortable when surrounded by others. When it was unavoidable it would cause her to get slightly claustrophobic. An example of this quirky behaviour was her taking the stairs rather than using the lift. It would be quite some time before Katie would finally get to grips with Mandy's delusional episodes as we called them. Mandy's mother Deborah was diagnosed with Schizophrenia and unsurprisingly she wondered if there was a link. When Katie told the doctor of her concerns he told her that her daughter was just being a difficult teen and held the opinion that she would grow out of it as it was a hormone thing. What a clever man! When finally examined our Mandy was visibly disappointed to learn that there was actually nothing wrong with her. Had there been a problem everyone would have to be attentive but now she was undeserving of special status. Mandy was such an attention seeker that if she had known about Munchhausen disease she would become a regular at the Vicky hospital. Thankfully she wouldn't be wasting their time on this fantasy girl.

Eventually Mandy would meet Steve. He would give her the attention she craved for and leave us to get on with our own lives. After a while Mandy did settle down so it appears that the diagnosis about it being hormonal was right. She sorted herself out and at the first opportunity she and Steve pissed off to Dublin. Apart from rare family get togethers such as at funerals I was never to see Mandy again. From there on she had all the privacy she could need and seemed happy in her new skin. Unfortunately the same couldn't be said for her sister Trina. Trina was in a bad way. She had about this time been arrested for committing a lewd act in the men's toilets in Sauchiehall Street. What really pissed her off was that she had been fined for giving this guy a blow job that she never got paid for. It appeared that her cover was blown, if that is the apt description, before she was paid for her services.

Trina didn't have a good life. Following in her mother's footsteps she was pregnant at just seventeen years of age. Then, again and again with dreary predictability the wheel of fate continued to spin. The cycle was not going to be broken and in turn Trina was to find her own daughter pregnant at the same early age. This was now third generation suffering the vicious cycle of deprivation and lack of direction. Wearily we wait to see if the seventeen year itch will encroach on the next child's life.

Trina had been evicted from her most recent apartment on account of her being behind - seriously behind, in her rent obligations. She had been receiving rent cheques from the housing office. However, instead of using it to pay the rent she was jacking it up her arm. Philosophical about her fall from grace she claimed to be glad to leave the shit hole as it only plagued her with bad memories anyway.

Two months earlier she and Paul, her equally dumb boyfriend, had got themselves into a bit of bother. The pair had stopped paying their drug dealers. When these two guys decided to pay Paul and Trina a visit things got heavy. As soon as Paul opened the door his feet left the ground as he received a Glasgow kiss (head butt). His nose was spread half way across his face. The hallway was covered in his blood and her boyfriend was yelping like a baby. The luckless debtor was then roughly dragged to his feet and then knocked down again. That was not the end of their ordeal for their two attackers were just warming up. The unwanted visitors had only just begun to show that they meant business. Terrified, Trina was crouching down behind the couch in a futile attempt at making herself scarce. Whatever, the sniffles coming from her pathetic little gob - didn't go unnoticed by the thugs. The smaller of the two pulled the sofa out and reaching behind it he yanked Trina up by grabbing a fistful of her hair. It was only when he punched her in the face with a clenched fist that she started screaming that she had 20 quid in her purse.

Her attacker was demented, 'Twenty fucking quid? Are you fucking kidding me?' the big bloke screamed. 'You owe me £200!'

They could see the state of the place. The apartment was an empty shell. It was typical of junkies to sell everything they possessed or had borrowed to chase the next buzz. Their brutish visitors grabbed Trina and despite her struggles they tied the terrified teenager to the flat's radiator. Wailing piteously she begged them not to rape her but her pleas went unheeded. Tearing her dress upwards they dragged Trina's underwear down and then in turn they then took advantage of her helplessness. This was not so much as satiating their physical needs. It was all about power and humiliation. As one entered her from behind, the smallest of her attackers grabbed a fistful of the unfortunate victim's hair and proceeded to use her mouth to masturbate until he ejaculated.

Not surprisingly Trina throughout all this was out of her mind. In the meantime her feller was feebly watching what was happening to his partner. As he did so he whined and protested but he was inwardly hoping that this visit was to be the settling of the debt. He fondly thought that the attack would be compensation for the £200 they owed the drug dealers. Wrong, very wrong!

As soon as the two finished what they felt they had to do to Trina the attackers grabbed Paul and threw him bodily out of the first storey tenement window. They didn't even bother opening it as they did so. Her boyfriend junkie was not having a good day. It could best be described as an Angus horribilis. A charitable Samaritan who happened to be passing at the moment he hit the pavement called an ambulance. It was there in a jiffy as the ambulance crew must have called to pay their respects on several earlier occasions. There and then the broken and distressed laddie was whisked off to the hospital repair department. He was treated for a broken nose, two broken legs and a dislocated shoulder. Interestingly, before the ambulance was called, five people witnessed what was happening but walked on by: See nothing, hear nothing, and say nothing. No one wanted to get involved in a drug addict's self-inflicted woes.

The two marauders left the distraught Trina tied to the radiator and before leaving threatened their return at a later date for moneys due. Their final remark was that what had happened on this occasion was a walk in the park compared with what they could expect if the owed money wasn't handed over. Such was their self confidence they brazenly left the couple's door wide open as they sauntered on their way.

Trina wasn't to be on her own for very long. After receiving an anonymous call or perhaps liaising with the emergency service a couple of uniformed cops appeared at the still open door. Understandably they where looking for explanations. The cops could clearly see that Trina was distraught as they untied her. The police officers were thoughtful enough to turn their backs as she reclaimed her torn underwear and her modesty. It wasn't the best of moments for Trina to appear dignified. She stunk of piss as she had wet herself through fear. She told the officers what she knew. This didn't amount to much. Two complete strangers had done this to her and she wasn't sure why? It was a feeble attempt to convince the officers that it was a case of mistaken identity. Perhaps this was due to their only having been in the flat for eight weeks?

She didn't tell the police she had been raped and abused. Probably there was little need to. As she was on record for having prostituted herself in the past she wasn't up there when it came to probity or credibility. Glasgow's cops knew exactly what had happened and why it had happened, for it was a common occurrence. If the truth be known they couldn't give a shit. Their attitude seemed to be that such victims set themselves up for it. Whatever the intention to investigate, and pursue, the couple's attackers; their hands were tied. The victims were unlikely to appear as witnesses. They knew before they took statements that they would receive the same bullshit from her partner. Paul was under no illusions. If this was what he got for a £200 outstanding bill what he would get for grassing didn't bear thinking about.

Paul would suffer from severe amnesia. He would be completely in the dark as to why two complete strangers would burst into his apartment and beat shit out of him before hurling him through a closed window. Trina decided it might just be a good time to put blue water between her and her partner Paul. After all, in her mind she was without fault. He should never have ticked the stuff. Sure she shared it with him but hadn't she done him some favours in return. He owed her.

The problem was worsened because the family was disinterested. Their attitude was similar to that of the policemen. Furthermore, they knew she was on the game and were well aware that she was dishonest to the marrow of her bones. When visiting family she literally had to be searched before she left to go on to wherever she was going. You couldn't even trust her to go to the toilet as en route you would find her in the kitchen eyes eying anything up that she thought might usefully be lifted.

Trina had hit rock bottom and as far as Aunt Katie was concerned her attempts at helping her daughter had come to nothing. You can't help someone who is unprepared to help themselves. Her mother washed her hands of her. She had reached the point that she would no more than shrug if she heard that Trina was on the streets selling herself. My mother took pity on her as she had been through all the drug-related dramas with Alfie. She knew well what she was letting herself in for when reluctantly she offered her an olive branch. Trina had just about enough savvy to take it.

Chapter 11
Trick and treat Trina

Trina from there on would become a permanent fixture in our lives for awhile. The upside of things for me for me was our never seeing much of Aunt Katie during that period. Every cloud has a silver lining. Trina knew Mother well and she knew that staying with Mother was not going to be a smooth ride. At the beginning our guest was pretty much followed everywhere around the house and was on lock-down. Trina knew that following the altercation at her flat she had no choice but to keep her head down. Under no illusions she was grateful to her aunt for the security and fresh start opportunity. For added security Madeline would do the return trip with Trina to the chemist when picking up her daily shot of methadone. Back at my mother's she was under curfew and knew better than to step out of line. She was aware that she had little choice but to get her life back in order. However pathetic it might be it was after all was said and done her life.

It was on a late Saturday night that Trina confided in me. She told me stories about her experiences with clients whom she described as her Johns. For the majority of encounters the sexual coupling was casual and over in minutes. Then as now there was a scare about the Aids virus. Taking precautions was advised but wearing a condom is not popular with the men, especially when paying for a blow job. Either way or whatever their inclinations it wasn't unusual for clients to offer Trina little extra money to ride her bareback. The description was new to me and I was unknowing about what she was talking about. Riding her bareback? Sensing my confusion she explained that it was shagging without a condom. Her punters lived for the risk and she lived for the brown sugar and so Trina was happy to oblige for the extra money that was so casually offered.

She said that a lot of the punters were obviously married but she didn't see that as being her concern. Trina went on to explain that, due to concerns over health issues, the price of gobbles (blow jobs) went up. As she warmed to the topic that evening she conceded that she actually derived pleasure from experiencing paid for gratuitous sex. I suppose it owed much to her otherwise bereft existence that she enjoyed the power that comes with controlling the occasion when giving her client a blow job. Likely, as she got on with what she was engaged to do and opened up the guy's trousers she got a big as kick out of retrieving his manhood, bringing him to arousal if he was not already there and offhandedly sucking him off as did the punter. Inevitably there would be the orgasm to contend with. Whoever she was servicing would orgasm and spurt his cum all over her face. This for her was part of the scene so to speak. If she was lucky she would afterwards be passed a tissue to wipe the flow from her stained face. Candidly she went on to say that when her punters were fully aroused they were adrenalin charged and shame wasn't part of the theatre. It is the world's oldest profession and Trina wasn't getting any younger.

Her month long stay with us was illuminating. I learnt a lot about compassion, there was empathy and I learnt also not to be judgemental. We all find our own ways to survive difficult situations and so did Trina. She did it her way. Survival is also a basic skill and Trina was doing whatever was necessary to keep herself alive. It was unfortunate for her that she got a flat in nearby Gorbals. The council treated as so much rubbish. The town hall mandarins tossed Trina into a foul hovel and they likely hoped fervently that she would overdose and they could rid themselves of her. Mother had been putting to one side crappy bits of furniture. Shona and Deborah and I helped the fallen woman to move to her new fleapit. We two were up and down half the morning, moving and humping her stuff and gagging every time we used the lifts and the landings, such was the stench of human piss and excrement.

With the little we had brought with us placed where we thought was best we took a despairing look around at her new bleak damp ridden home. Yes, of course we tried to look on the bright side of things. There was the usual shit: 'Hey, it's cool' and 'at least it is your own place. '

We would then comment on the need for a coat of paint but leaving aside such pleasantries we couldn't wait to get out into the fresh air. Despite reassurances of keeping in touch with Trina none of us had the slightest intention of ever returning. I can remember Shona being really and truly pissed off. I recall her saying that after all the humping stuff up there the bitch wasn't even likely to live there. It was just a convenient Giro-drop. Social security cheques are commonplace but it was necessary to have an address. Without it, scrounging money from the local authority was impossible. If a tenant moved into unfurnished accommodation then the council would provide a loan to purchase bare necessities. Instead of buying furniture they used the money to fund their smack habit and so the cycle goes on. Trina went back to her old ways. She was taking the council for fools and when it was apparent that she was not playing by the rules they decided she was taking the piss and again they evicted her.

Aunt Katie was now back on the scene and the alcohol debauchery would commence. Never again did any of us help that bitch again. My mother felt guilty or at least that's what she said. In her opinion Trina had needed more time and support. Little did she know Trina couldn't wait to get away from her. Fair play to my mother for doing what she thought best but she could be a living nightmare to live with and no one knew that better than I did. Trina had completely lost her way in life and many years would pass before she recovered. It is to her credit that eventually she did so. It has to be the desire to get back on one's feet on one's own part. Aunt Katie had nurtured Trina's daughter Tara for some years. She accepted the situation but well knew that the 'life' Trina was living was no place for a child. Trina went to the dole to declare herself homeless and the cycle began again. Soon there would be a new shit hole, more loans, prostitution, drug taking, debasement; life was hell and the drudgery for Trina droned on and on.

When Trina's daughter Tara was five years old her surrogate mother felt it was time for the youngster to be permanently reunited with her biological mother. By this time Trina had been through rehab and had been sober for six months or so we were led to believe. In the world free of fantasy she had been in rehab for three months. On the day of her release she was shouting up at Maddie's window asking if she knew anybody who might have any kit. Maddie never took that road so Tara went to live with her surrogate mother and at this point most of the family lived in the south side of Glasgow.

Chapter 12
When a phone call changes a life

It was a day when Shona took a phone call that would change her life, and ours forever. It was just a regular Saturday afternoon and she was channel-hopping from her sprawled position on the settee. Shona was fragile that day as she and Maddie had partied the evening before and had got somewhat bladdered. Alone in the house, Maddie was at work and Aunt Bella was with her friends attending their ritual Saturday afternoon session at the Mecca bingo hall.

Taking the call, the surprised Shona recognised the voice of her cousin, Teddy. He wanted to see her like now, but he was mystifyingly vague as to the reasons why; it was important that she join him. It was something of a challenge. Her cousin lived nearby in South-east London in Peckham, which is Del Boy's manor. The artful dodger and ever aspiring hapless entrepreneur through the TV series put Peckham on the map.

Teddy made it crystal clear that her visit was important and that without delay she should visit his flat. He had something very important chopping from one channel to another. Shona accepted his invitation and sense of urgency at face value and she told him she would be with him soon. Shona was of course intrigued and popping a couple of Paracetamol in an attempt to feel normal she began to organise herself to go on her way. As she did so she tried to decipher Teddy's words and tone to gauge whether he was sounding up or down. She didn't have any answers to her mind games and as she showered she thought to herself she would find out soon enough.

Shona and Maddie kept her cousin's company often. Teddy was Peckham born and bred. His dialect, mannerisms and accent were pure Cockney. It was not the Estuary English so commonplace now and taken to be the London lingo today. Their cousin had bright ginger hair and he had heard all the usual remarks about his colourful top. A likeable guy, he seemed to know just about everybody in South East London. As he worked as a postman it wouldn't be unheard of to find him propping up the bar on afternoons. He would finish his round early and from there on his life could be carefree. If he was not in his local then he would be off loading his earnings at the local bookies where he claimed to have an insider's knowledge when backing horses. Evidently he was not inside far enough.

Teddy was a disciplined gambler who at least understood the philosophy of only betting what you can afford to lose. He always understood his limits. Teddy was what some might call a wigger. That is a white European who having turned his back on his own kind thinks and acts as if he is black. Shona often said she wasn't sure if he was taking the piss when he was around his Jamaican mates and lamenting wa'appun (what's happening what's going down bredda (brother)). He could switch from cockney to the hip hop gangsta vernacular no problem. Teddy wore ridiculously baggy pants that were usually half way done his arse. My cousin's appearance looked to me as if he needed a good shit or already had had one. He was constantly giving high fives whilst sauntering and snapping his fingers. Teddy was not so much as a Del Boy as a Delroy.

His mother was my Aunt Sheila, she was a lady who was profoundly deaf and had been sent to a school for the deaf in Glasgow as a child. That is where she would meet her future pathetic excuse for a husband. I think she resented my grandmother for sending her there. Basically a boarding school, she lived in as a boarder throughout the week and only came home at the weekends. My gran never had time for her. I think the problem was my grandmother could not communicate with her daughter and her daughter's company exasperated her. Sure she knew a few of the universal signs but she never attempted to try and learn sign language. The first time I visited my aunt's house the lights kept going off and then on. This carried ritual on the whole time I was present.

One day curiosity got the better of me. I asked Teddy if they had a problem with their electricity. I felt a complete fool when he explained that, as his mother couldn't hear the door bell, the lights were flicked to indicate someone was at the door. Once explained it made complete sense but I was embarrassed as I had seen the comings and goings and I had never twigged.

The complexions of Aunt Sheila had Teddy, Tanya and Sarah was ghostly white which contrasted greatly with their bright ginger hair. It was not as bad for the girls as makeup could compensate but for Teddy he looked like the matchstick boy - on fire. My aunt's husband was classed as a mute but it was a strangely selective affliction. When he was at the dole office he was as deaf as a doorpost but when socialising, provided you raised your voice a little, he could follow easily enough. He could certainly hear the sound of a whisky bottle opening or a fizzy can pull being jerked.

One of a large family the man was work shy. He played the social security system and received more on benefits than he would have earned as an unskilled worker. It was hardly rocket science why he took the lazy option. The work-shy character spent most of his days in the bookies when he wasn't in Sainsbury's stealing the dinner. Shona says the hands would go up in favour of dinner tonight. Then she and my uncle would go on their cashless shopping expeditions and return with the goods.

On the few occasions when they got caught red-handed the pair would certainly use their disability in their favour. They would literally act dumb and pretend they didn't understand. Waving their arms around would purposely let it be known that they were angry. Sure they were bloody angry - for being caught. Their heavy handed sign language was intended to intimidate. After all the fuss and to-do at the stores they visited they were never formally arrested and usually they received a written caution.

With her familiarity of the family Shona wasn't exactly his biggest fan. She vehemently denounced him as a scrounging knob head constantly whining for a cigarette or a couple of quid. Cute as in monkey he was too shrewd to allow a penny to slip by. His memory lapses were as profound as his hearing loss when he owed someone money. She often reminded me of Mandy. She loved attention and took it in whatever formed it was offered. She and her sister attended a school attached to a convent. She didn't have a happy time at all with the penguins and was caned frequently. In England, the controlling mechanism was detention. It had a negative effect on my cousin because she started to hate school with a vengeance. Such schools are run by severe disciplinarians and their way of doing things was not Tanya's way of doing things. Shona had a zest for life and her enthusiasm was endearing but it was invariably exhausting. My sister was without doubt, one of the most tactless people that I had ever met. Like my gran she certainly told it like it is. This was a trait that a lot of female members in my family seemed to have inherited.

Teddy's friend Benson, or Ben as he was known, hailed from, Ghana. A terrific guy, he was gentlemanly and avoided using cockney slang. He disregarded the term coloured as he said it was the inside that counts. His friends referred to him as Malteser. This was on account of his being white on the inside and black on the outside.

Benson lived in affluent Dulwich Village. The Ghanaian had been adopted as a baby by a wealthy white couple after his parents returned to their home country. It was a lucky break for him. He was now doing well at Camberwell College and was at this time on his way for a Business Diploma. Initially, Shona said she thought of Teddy and Ben as the Odd Couple. As she got to know Teddy better she would see beyond his showy facade and see him in a different light. Teddy was in fact quite studious and he spent many a long hour debating David Icke and the Illuminati. He loved everything to do with the conspiracy theories.

My aunt and her husband, Uncle Malcolm wouldn't normally tolerate those of different race to their own. Ben was the exception to this unwritten rule. It could be said that he was their token black friend to establish their credentials as non-racist. Being polite and courteous, Ben had gone the extra mile and he had impressed them by learning the sign language alphabet. One day, a peculiar and unexpected incident took place. After the event Aunt Sheila never spoke to my sister Madeline ever again.

As Madeline and Ben worked near to each other and they often lunched together the two became more than friends but having said that they were not lovers. There was certainly affection between them. If you want to rephrase that to lust then feel free to allow your imagination to go where it will. Maddie certainly did.

One thing that could be said for my sister was she was a crutch watcher. In the company of Ben she found her eyes wandering on more than one occasion. Well, she was curious as she had heard that all coloureds are well hung. Her interest revealed a body language that Ben well understood. Her interest in him, or at least a certain section of his anatomy, had quite an aphrodisiacal affect on the more animalistic side of his nature. In order to see her reaction he would jerk his manhood when he knew she was looking at him down there. Well they say the quickest way to get a woman into bed is to make her laugh and Ben was good at making his would-be paramour laugh.

'Is it true what is said about you guys,' she teased one afternoon. It was a brazen and provocative question as, sitting a little apart from the others in their group the pair communicated in sweet nothings.

'That's for me to know and it is for you to find out,' he winked suggestively.

Oh for a challenge and how Maddie loved challenge given the opportunity. Sex of course didn't come into it, or that was as she would have it. Only the challenge mattered. It was a 'dare you' scenario that was developing. Waiting for his response Maddie held Ben's challenging gaze as they enjoyed a quiet bistro session together.

Behind them they could hear the sound of chairs and tables being moved about. From what conversation Maddie and Ben could hear the others in their company were now intent on drifting back to Teddy's place. This wasn't quite the place or opportunity that the amorous pair had in mind for their hoped for voyage of sexual discovery. In the 'catch up later with you parting melee, Maddie and the highly aroused and anticipatory Ben they went blithely on their own sweet romantic way.

'Shush,' Maddie whispered in a conspiratorial whisper as she gently turned the key in the front door lock of Aunt Sheila's home. Her home was conveniently situated not too far away from the party venue. With Itchy pants standing expectantly behind Maddie, Ben nodded his approval as the door silently edged open. The amorous and eager couple then sneakily tiptoed their way up the stairs to the bedroom where Maddie was known to kip down. On this occasion sleep was the last thing on the mind of the seductress. As the bedroom door closed behind them the pair paused just long enough to satisfy themselves that their arrival had not been noticed by Aunt Sheila downstairs. She might be doing chores or catching up on the soaps. Whatever, Sheila was blissfully unaware of the presence of Maddie and Ben in the upstairs bedroom.

With her eyes gleaming with lust Maddie fell into Ben's embrace. With barely a nod in the direction of decency the horny little wench was now excruciatingly aware of the physical effect that she was having on her ebony-skinned seducer. The twitching bulge in Ben's trousers was begging for release in more ways than one.

'Fuck the foreplay' she thought to herself.

Ben's thoughts evidently mirrored her own. While she quickly dismantled the holding apparatus of his jeans, Ben's hands were groping her breasts. In those breezy bouncy days of spring-like bloom there was little need for the wearing of bras. His wandering hands left him little time to wonder and sure enough they were real and they were firm.

This romantic encounter was all too much for Maddie. As fast as she unfastened Ben's belt she deftly undid her own. With a kick of her feet that would have earned the undying praise of a barrio tango dancer my sister's discarded jeans were quickly sent into orbit and then followed into oblivion by her knickers.

From knickers to high kickers the pair of them, without a thought in their minds save for their lust, the two threw caution to the winds. When a few moments later the bedroom door handle gently turned Maddie's ankles were keeping the company of Ben's ears and she was enjoying the white knuckle ride of her life.

This was the fastest moment in history that a maiden's deflowering morphed into deflation. The Bank of England would have given the two a round of applause. There stood my aunt Sheila with a face incandescent with naked fury. The equally naked and rudely splayed not to mention shamed Maddie was mortified. It appeared that Sheila had felt vibrations through the floor and decided to investigate. An earthquake perhaps, anything but not on God's earth a black man with a prong the size of Nelson's Column giving her niece a good seeing to.

Deaf people can really bellow and Sheila screamed her head off like she was demented. Her language would have done a trooper proud. Launching herself across the bedroom, Maddie's brief encounter with justice was about to get colourful. In this respect we are not talking of Ben's ebony black skin. Grabbing Maddie by her hair she manhandled her naked niece down the stairs and hurled her into the street. Benson was right behind her but fortunately in his case had just enough time and wit to throw his clothes back on. He had thoughtfully and gallantly grabbed Maddie's T-shirt thinking that she would have to wear something to give her a little modesty. It was a little late for that.

Fortunately for the two, Teddy's flat was nearby. When the disgraced and publicly humiliated pair appeared at his door they had no option but to come clean. Everyone there was in stitches. The shrieking, chortling and ribald remarks were the icing on the cake for the disgraced couple. Does it get any worse?

'I think you will need a stiff one,' chortled the effervescent Teddy.

Maddie told me that she was secretly shitting herself. She had after her standing and her future to think about. This small imprudent act was to cast its shadows over the years that lay ahead of her. Maddie knew that the next time the bitch aka Sheila was in Scotland the world and his wife would know about the fall from grace and how embarrassing would that be. She had no regrets about being banged by Ben. It was the circumstances in which she had been caught in flagrant indelicto. She had not even had the satisfaction of seeing their horny sex through to an earth moving curtain call. Having been so far shagged in every position known to man nothing now was new to Maddie. This occasion was a bit of a break from tradition and she had little to show for it other than the pre-orgasm. Hey, she was philosophical about it and took the view that what was done was done.

The next time Malcolm saw Maddie he called her a whore and said she wasn't fit to breathe the same air as he and his wife Sheila. Maddie's response was to laugh in his face. There was some concern as Malcolm was well built and he could easily have decked Maddie. Thankfully for her looks he just turned his back on her. Aunt Sheila would indeed tell my mother at a later date. Uncle Malcolm was always blaming black people for the area's deterioration. His feelings did not get any better towards our coloured friends when his wife was mugged by coloureds. It would happen to her on three occasions and all of the muggings occurred in the borough of Peckham.

There was not a person in the whole of Peckham that did not hear my uncle's screams when he was told of the third attack on his wife. My cousin Teddy said all he could do was stop him leaving the front door with his hammer intent on finding those black bastards and caving their skulls. After some persuasion he passed out drunk on the sofa.

He now thought it was his fault as what sort of man would allow his wife to walk about after dark? He knew Sheila, especially due to her being deaf, made her especially vulnerable but he was too proud to apologise. His failing was a decision that he would regret for the rest of his life. He was Scottish and proud of it. He very much reminded one of the cartoon character Hagar the Viking. The Scots usually tell you of their land's great inventors and writers in equal proportion to their slagging the English about their football. Malcolm's views on English beer were hardly complimentary. The pub regulars ignored him. As long as you were Caucasian he was considered harmless. A devout Celtic football team supporter it was a no-brainer for Teddy to follow in his dad's footsteps.

On this occasion Shona was summoned to Teddy's place as a matter of urgency and pacing the floorboards waiting for her, Teddy wasn't sure how to handle the situation. It was clear that he had been weeping and her arrival couldn't be far off. He had earlier taken a call from

Aunt Martha and had been tasked with telling Shona that her sister Deborah had died. Knowing that Maddie was of emotional nature he knew it wouldn't be easy to console her. Thinking a half ounce of weed might help to calm the coming storm he went to see a mate. On his way he bought a shed load of wine and then on returning to his home he waited for the knock on the door he was dreading.

Teddy must have checked the windows a dozen times. He finally decided a plan of action was what was needed. Furiously he began to roll spliffs and after what seemed like an eternity Shona appeared at his front door. Welcoming his visitor with the usual peck on the cheek he tried to appear nonchalant but she could see his turmoil at first glance. His eyes were pink and shrivelled and if anything he looked slightly demonic.

Poor Shona, she had been expecting an afternoon of fun and maybe a few games of pool in the pub. The last thing she expected was to see her cousin so distraught. Taking her coat, Teddy opened the wine and he then poured a glass for each of them.

'I don't how to say this, Shona. In fact, there isn't a good way to say it. I am sorry, so sorry. I know it will break your heart but Deborah has passed over. She was found this morning.'

As soon as he uttered the fateful words he collapsed into sobs. Shona's face as he did so was stone-faced blank. What she had just heard was too surreal for her to grasp its true meaning. Taking a long drawn out drag of the spliff she tossed the contents of the wine glass down her neck. She then sat motionless and stared without seeing. She later told me that it was if her mind was not registering what Teddy had just spoken. Teddy was in just as bad a state and weeping he was now practically strangling her with embraces. She could feel his tears mingling with her own as they began to sob.

The tears flowed and would do so regardless of passing of time. After awhile there was an attempt by both at the need to come to terms with the news. Neither she nor Teddy spoke but the spliffs continued to pass from hand to hand as did the glasses of wine. Teddy had chosen an Eagles track for background solace. Shona later confided that she could never again listen to the band's melodies without filling up.

The two for seemingly an eternity sat there gripping their glasses. What then occurred was the weirdest thing that had either had ever experienced. Shona, for some reason she could never explain, found herself inexplicably attracted to one of the room's corners. It was an attraction that was beyond her experience. It was a fixation with that particular corner of the room. It was as if she was mesmerised. Her attention was drawn to this particular corner as if a form of possession had transcended and was now controlling events. Her entire being experienced a strangeness that was totally beyond description. Shona's body was engulfed by a tingling sensation as energy pulsated from the corner. There was magnetism to it, a concentration that was omnipotent. It was neither evil nor saintly, it was just present yet at the same time it was unearthly. There was no mistaking the eeriness of her sister's presence.

My sister said she could never find the words to express the sensations she felt in the knowledge that Deborah was there. She was as present as was Teddy, and she was adamant that the sensation, never before experienced, was unrelated to either the wine or the weed.

Teddy at the time could see that Shona was fixated with something that he himself was clueless about. Whatever it was there was no questioning her focused concentration on the room's corner

He wasn't exactly sitting in the West Wing of the White House. Before she got a chance to explain what she was experiencing, the strange sensations flooding over her, Teddy did it for her. Without any collaboration between the two of them he too was now sharing the same weird sensations. This would disprove any possibility of their being collaboration or the visitation being related to any other cause. He afterwards described the same feelings. His skin prickled and the hairs on the nape of his neck stood upright. The sensations were purely involuntary as the two felt the overwhelming presence of Deborah. She was unseen but there was no mistaking her presence. It was terribly and shockingly real for both of them.

Deborah and Teddy even today and long after the event firmly believe that Deborah had come to say her final goodbye to them. She had done so in her own way as to reassure them that she was in death only in a mortal sense. Maddie and Shona would later return to Glasgow separately. A great sadness had descended on them. It was with a heart as heavy as a boulder that Maddie would board the train for Glasgow Central Station.

Shona decided that she and Teddy would take the coach to Glasgow. It was a grim occasion for Shona as at the time she was afflicted by chicken-pox and was covered head to toe in calamine lotion. It concerned her not that she looked a sight for sore eyes. It didn't matter to her that the curiosity of passengers' stares went far beyond merely rude glances. Having to deal with her sister's loss was far more distracting than was the attention she was getting. Returning to Glasgow for her sister's funeral she knew that of all the heavy loads life had thrust on to her shoulders this was by far the heaviest burden of them all.

The usual practice on a National Express coach was you paid the driver upon boarding the bus. For reasons best known to himself the driver never asked Shona or Teddy for their fares. It was not an oversight for later, when carrying out a head count; he conspicuously failed to include them. It was as if these two passengers, Teddy and Shona were invisible. That couldn't have been easy given Shona's appearance. The two shrugged and consoled themselves that Deborah must have paid their fares.

Maddie was at the same time on her way home on the train. It was a six hour journey that in other circumstances was usually pleasant enough. The journey was pleasing and relaxing as the carriages clickety-clacked through the English and Scottish countryside. Like most passengers there were plenty of other pastimes to keep minds occupied. There were one's own thoughts, perhaps a book, a magazine or puzzles. Her journey that day was a trip through Hades. It was a never ending nightmare that was accompanied only by grief.

Maddie later told me that she wept through most of the journey and I could understand that. She said people would pass her and pause to ask if she was all right. Dumbly she would shake her head, too upset to even speak in return for their kindness. Apparently there had been a few interludes when she had been sobbing so much that she was losing her breath. This would aggravate her condition because then she would find herself beginning to panic which was a tipping point into hysteria. She couldn't bring herself to accept that her sister had died and as the song says, 'Why do the birds go on singing?

Don't they know it's the end of the world?'

She fully agreed that she must have had the appearance of someone under a Care in the Community order. Sometimes, in the midst of all the crying, she would recall the fun and crazy times that she and Deborah had had together. The two sisters had been to some real fun parties on many an occasion. When doing so they would get wasted and it would be then they would simply chill out listening to the music that was to their taste and mood.

Maddie's emotions were all over the place and she just cried unremittingly. Music tracks constantly interrupted her thoughts and one of them was one of Deborah's favourite songs. This was Seasons in the Sun sung by one of their favourite singers, Terry Jacks. As she listened to its heartbreaking lyrics she was painfully aware that she would never say a proper goodbye to her 'dear and trusted friend.'

This was no star trek journey that was for sure. Father had called Aunt Bella as Mother was not able to deal with what was going on around her. She took to her bed. She didn't take a drink but the doctor had been called and she reluctantly accepted the sedative offered. There was no fight in her. It was unnatural for a mother and a father to bury their child.

Mother was not a church going person. There was no holy water in our home although there was a crucifix evident. This was something of a show symbol and I supposed a way of showing respect to the Gran. For some bizarre reason Mother refused to keep a Bible in the house. If she had ever held any religious conviction then now was the ultimate test of faith. If my mother had the strength to do so we could be sure to hear her blaspheming but we never did. There was just the eerie stillness that descended like an emotional fog on a home that had so often been a place of good humour and gaiety. Only after Deborah's funeral did she remove the domestic ornaments depicting our Catholicism. These were banished to a drawer and would never see the light of day again.

Deborah's death caused a kaleidoscope of emotions and affected different family members in different ways. We all went through initial shock, the disbelief and denial but cold reality has a habit of slapping you very hard on the face. When it does then it brings you down to earth with a sickening thud.

After Father had telephoned Aunt Bella and he, had given her the grim news, she knew that any time soon Maddie would finish work. It fell on her to tell her of her sister's death. It was for certain the most disagreeable thing she had ever been called upon to do. Hearing Maddie's key turning in the door's lock she stiffened her shoulders and her resolve as she made a vain attempt at composing herself. She had prepared well for in sight was a box of Kleenex. At first glance Aunt Bella gave little away, although the invitation that Maddie take the weight off her feet might have raised a suspicion of sort. It was an unusual request for her to make.

Offering a perplexed Madeline a tissue the youngster politely accepted. Inwardly, a sixth sense perhaps, she knew that all was not right on this occasion. She sensed also that what she was about to hear would be life changing. Bella's normal amiability had deserted her. Sitting in her chair she was tightly clutching the box of tissues and on occasion dabbing at her swollen eyes. Inside she felt like collapsing in grief and letting the tears flow. Bella somehow kept her composure for Maddie's sake as she told my sister of the tragedy that had fallen on the family.

Maddie never responded by word or eye contact. Silently she listened quietly and then rising to her feet she walked with very steady tread in the direction of her bedroom. The impact of the revelation caused her to become zombie-like. Moments later Bella could hear the uncontrolled wailing coming from the bedroom. Only then did she allow herself to weep her own tears and for both there was the mantra, why.

Over the following days family and friends would come together and they would travel from as far as Australia for Deborah's funeral. Despite the re-unions, in some case after separations lasting years, it was far from being a joyous time. A visit from the priest and the sisters of mercy only added to the sombre mood of the occasion. Father Mark sat and read Mary Stevenson's Footprints in the Sand. 'During your times of trial and suffering / When you see only one set of footprints / It was then that I carried you.'

The priest had an irritating habit of rubbing his palms together as if he was very cold. Gran had asked Father Mark to visit the grieving family as a mark of respect. It was all for show. Mother didn't want or need the ecclesiastics and she pretty much ignored the minister. She was in abstemious mood too and far too consumed by grief to trust herself with alcohol. That at least was one blessing bestowed upon the family.

Alfie and I went to the train station to meet up with Madeline whilst Shona and Teddy intended to take a taxi home from the bus station. We decided that we would go to Glasgow's Central Station but not before downing a couple of jars on the way.

Maddie, looking like shit, stepped off the train. She was clearly a long way from being as tidy in her appearance as she was known to be. She normally took pride in her appearance but it was plain to see that she didn't give a flying fuck whatever anyone might have thought for her dishevelment.

Of course we were happy to see her but we were also gutted by the circumstances of our doing so. We had all missed Maddie whilst she had been in London. What we hadn't realised was that only one of the sister's would return to London whilst the other would remain permanently in Glasgow. Between us it was decided that it would be too depressing to return home and we all ploughed into the pub. As a group we were respectful and we didn't overdo things. We also knew that my mother was looking forward to seeing Maddie. There was enough upset as it was without adding further to it.

Teddy and Shona would be arriving home soon too and there would be need for solace. We all headed to the shops and we bought some beers. Thinking it might be a tad insensitive to carry them home we stashed them at Andrea's house. We would all return later for a bit of a get together but having taken care of the future there was now the present to look out for. The house when we got there was strangely quiet. Father was nowhere to be seen but we knew where we would likely find him. He would be drowning his sorrows in his local bar. Dad had been closer to Deborah than his other daughters. One of his lowest moments was when he would be called upon to identify his daughter resting on a slab of concrete. Life had been short and cruel for Debs but at least we could console ourselves that she was now asleep and finally at peace.

Father would ask Alfie to go and get him a sedative to calm his nerves. Mother was feigning sleep for I don't think she could cope with what was going on around her. It was far too much to bear and she opted for the ostrich way by burying her head not in the sand but in her grief. It was not a healthy atmosphere and we as a group decided to turn about heel and head off to Andrea's house. Once there we could toast Deborah's eternal happiness in the afterlife. We tried not to dwell too much on our troubles. Nobody was brave enough to say Deborah's name in case it set someone off. We just acted as if it was a little get together.

As is traditional for Catholics to view the dead before interment we were ushered into the Chapel of Rest. Shona couldn't bring herself to look into the coffin. Unfortunately, my aunt Martha took her to one side and said she was being very disrespectful to Mother and that she should say her last goodbye. Shona later told me she wished she had stuck to her guns and not been emotionally blackmailed into seeing her sister in a body bag. She has never attended a funeral since. Shona said her sister looked almost yellow and when she bent to kiss her forehead it was like kissing stone.

The next few days were in limbo and we were at the stage where you just want it to be all over. We hung around for days waiting for the cremation. This was the preferred option as Deborah had a terrible fear of the dark. The weather on the day of the final goodbye didn't help. Mother predicted that it would rain as if somehow it was a sign from God that not all was well with the world. It did.

After the service we headed back to my aunt's house that was soon stuffed to the doors with family and close friends. I felt nauseous watching these people tuck into homemade pie and veg. They were laughing like drains as if it was just another shindig. I wanted to stand and swear, 'What the fuck, how can you bear to eat when we have just incinerated my sister?'

There were many cousins who were present that very sad day. Mandy had arrived from England with her new boyfriend on her arm. Teddy and his sisters Sarah and Tanya arrived from London with Aunt Sheila and their father Malcolm. There was family from Edinburgh and relatives who appeared from the far corner. Deborah was well liked and deeply loved.

Considering why we were all together there was a happy atmosphere and it all went off just as we would have wished it and without drama. Sarah, Aunt Sheila's eldest daughter, stopped the music and asked us to join her in prayer. That suggestion was a little too theatrical for everyone's taste. A few called out for her to go and fuck herself and the volume was turned up to drown out any likely protests.

Yes, it was loud and Andrea would have to do some apologising to her neighbours in the morning. For now that was neither her concern nor ours. Sarah took the ribald rebuffs in good spirit, gave up any idea of a prayer meeting and proceeded to dance her feet off. Unlike Tanya, uppity Sarah was well mannered and liked to think herself that bit higher than most of us. A complete and utter snob she rented a flat in Peckham postcode SE 15. The postman once knocked on her door and reminded her that she was not living in the SE 22 area.

Her friends, when sending cards, thought she lived in Dulwich. She was embarrassed to admit that in fact she lived in Peckham. There she was a silver service waitress. I gather this occupation is what inspired her delusions of grandeur.

Sarah was hardly the angel she made herself out to be. She had once been caught in a sexually compromising position with Teddy's mate Ewan. Fortunately, it was the father and not the mother who had caught the two of them enjoying a little slap and tickle. When Aunt Sheila discovered that Sarah had been on the pill since she was nineteen years of age, she went ballistic and hurled all her stuff out of the door.

Sarah would spend most of her unexpected freedom away from her home and she was soon to move in with her lover. Ewan was a nice enough Irish guy who was almost twenty years older than his girlfriend. It was the age difference between them that possibly irked my aunt. Her Irishman was not a bad catch. A talented carpenter he had lived in London for a long time and his reputation kept him busy. Also an enthusiastic whiskey drinker he was forever jovially arguing with Teddy and claiming that Irish whiskey was better than Scots whisky. Teddy and Ewan had become friends three years earlier when Teddy had done a few days labouring on a building site at the Elephant and Castle.

Shona was to form a close friendship with Sarah but realised soon afterwards that her friend was high-minded, too high maintenance and something of a diva. The cordial relationship was not to last long. She was to afterwards give Sarah a wide berth.

One day, out of the blue, Sarah called Shona and asked for her company that day. Her explanation was that she had to go to hospital and they would not release her unless she had someone with her. Shona agreed to tag along as her Ewan was unwell and coincidentally he was in the same hospital with a collapsed lung. Once at the hospital it did not take a rocket scientist to realise that they were in the department where abortions are carried out.

It was wrongly thought that Ewan had a low sperm count and there had never been a need for them to take precautions. This was a mistake for his little swimmers had been heading up the right channel and they were docking at the right wharfs. Whilst at the hospital Shona took opportunity to visit her friend's other half. A little obtuse and embarrassed about her reason for being there she made her excuses and took the quick exit.

When Sarah was released hours later it was Shona who was there for her and none of her fancy Chigwell friends. This would not be the last time that Shona would accompany her to hospital and the reasons for the visits mortified Shona. Ewan had absentmindedly forgotten that he had somehow caught the herpes disease long before the two had met. It had been thought it had been successfully treated but the venereal infection had only been dormant. Sarah had to endure visits to the clap clinic and didn't Shona love Sarah's humiliating fall from grace.

Her friend had always looked down her nose on others yet now she was cringing inwardly and sitting uncomfortably on a bench with other carriers of venereal disease. After a while Sarah stopped asking Shona to accompany her and if anything she was from there on blanked by her cousin. Shona told that watching her cousin squirm at the clinic was enough enjoyment for her. Shona was not of malicious nature but I think uppity Sarah led with her chin and given the opportunity Shona delighted in taking a shot at it.

There were undoubted flaws in the family genes. Sheila's Malcolm had arrived home early one evening. He had then tiptoed upstairs to his daughter's bedroom. He fully expected to delight in his daughter's slumbers. Well, he was half right for the youngster sure enough was sleeping peacefully. Also in a dream world was Pete who was oblivious to the girl's father. Sitting beside the child's bed he was tossing himself off as he gazed at her sleeping face. Peter was ejected and was never again to set foot in the house.

Sarah later explained it was not the first time she had found Pete in her bedroom. There was an occasion when she had gone to bed wearing her pyjamas but when she awoke the following morning she was naked. She kept it to herself as she was thinking she might have imagined wearing her Jim-jams to bed. She kept her little secret for a long time and we felt that with her bulimia problems and her training at the time to be a cook was a strange career choice. However, she had over the years educated herself and had learnt to control her health issues. She learned to love food and in turn better respect what she was.

Chapter 13
Stevie gets it in

In the small hours the revellers attending Deborah's wake began to disperse. There were quite a few cousins at the party I had not seen in at least five years. At such gatherings you find yourself intrigued to know what they have been up to. Cousin Stevie was a character and we loved listening to his stories about what he got up to since he had moved to Leeds. Stevie had wonky eyes, one being brown and the other blue, a bit like David Bowie really. Steve was Uncle Charlie's eldest lad but father and son were anything but close. Steve was easily influenced and you can interpret that as naïve or dumb. His dark sandy hair always looked like it needed a good washing but even afterwards it looked as dirty as ever. He wasn't tall, slightly less than average at 5' 6" and he did have the strongest Glasgow accent imaginable.

Stevie was Grandmother's first grandchild. Always having a soft spot for him there was a big difference to the way she treated him compared to her more indifferent attitude towards Alfie. Her beloved Steve was often unemployed and like many others he had considered joining the British Army. No one took much notice of that ambition but Gran did. As soon as she heard of his intentions she put her foot hard down. There was no way on this earth that her young grandson was going to be a part of Thatcher's army. It was unthinkable that he would wear the Queen's uniform and to be sent to Ireland to fight in the troubles. Gran wasted no time to get that idea out of his head. She immediately contacted a friend of hers and secured Steve a job. There was just the one failing. The job opportunity was in Leeds. As far as Gran was concerned it could have been in Timbuktu. Anything was preferable to wrapping oneself in the butcher's apron to be used as cannon fodder in the British Army.

That was that settled and Stevie was soon packed off to Leeds. Satisfied, having secured digs and work for him she had put everything right again. She knew she would miss him being around the house but the sacrifice far outweighed the stress and worry if he had been sent to Ireland at the whim of the Iron Lady.

Stevie had an address to go to and he also had strict instructions to get a taxi straight there and to not go gallivanting. That was Gran's intention but it was not one he even considered honouring. The successful job applicant blithely thought that a pint never did anyone any harm. The problem was that for him one beer was no more than a meaningless expression. Predictably, he was to later roll up at his new digs as pissed as a newt. His new landlady was not impressed but charitably showed him to his room. When Stevie awake the following morning he wondered where the fuck he was and clambering from his bed he made his way down to the kitchen area.

There he found himself on the receiving end of a well-deserved torrent of abuse from his new landlady of whom it might be said he had but a vague recollection. As the distressed lady rambled and vented her frustration he idly started to consider working hard and making enough cash to enable him to lodge with a more obliging landlady. He did however keep his job appointment. He liked the idea of it and he was taken on as a painter and decorator.

Stevie had revealed that he had the crabs. This led to our asking how he had caught the condition. He told us. Having settled into his new job the day arrived when he and his mate Eric were called to one side. They were to be sent to decorate the home of a woman who appeared to live on her own. That in itself was hardly unusual but her behaviour towards the two tradesmen was extraordinary. She appeared to be perfectly normal and attired and greeted them both warmly and making them a drink before the two pulled on their overalls.

Later, the two painters and decorators were focusing on the work in hand when a sudden movement caught their eye. Through the open doorway of the room where they were working they could clearly see the reasonably attractive lady of the house in an adjoining room. Unlike her earlier appearance she was on this occasion wearing nothing else but her bra and panties. Her underwear was shall we say provocative.

If you have got it, flaunt it and it was it must be supposed her way of telling the two that she was up for it. It was no oversight on her part. The lady of the house wanted cock and she wanted it badly. There was just no way, those two virile young men were going to spend time in her home without receiving their bonus. If anything it might be assumed that the job was nothing more than a ruse to hook a couple of compliant studs. It must be said that if nothing else the damsel was of a charitable nature.

The gentle sex often complains of a lack of romanticism and foreplay. This lady was unlikely to share such sentiment. For goodness sake, didn't she realise that giving the guys the opportunity to remove her bra and panties and feast their eyes on what was on offer was part of the hardening process? We two sisters were paying rapt attention to Stevie's account of the interesting saga. Characteristically he told us like it was and he didn't pull punches because we were sisters rather than his buddies.

Stevie was asked, 'Well you don't get crabs off lavatory seats or by looking at a naked woman. What happened? How did you get the crabs?'

A little boyish banter took place, the woman client teased and pleased and generally let it be known that she was enjoying their compliments. The challenge was made and after she had removed her bra and panties it was clear that she wanted a good poking and fuck the foreplay. It was then that Stevie ruefully admitted that the reason for his ailment was agreeing to his working colleague giving the woman one first. It was not much a chivalrous gesture for his friend, who was not quite as quick to take advantage of the situation, was by this time already half undressed. There was no question of his enthusiasm for his erection spoke in a body language that left little need for sweet nothings in her ear.

The 'lady' blew kiss or two Stevie's way and her follow up wink suggested that he would be on the back burner for only a short time.

Off the amorous threesome went. Why not? Having earlier and quite unnecessarily showed the two her ultra feminine bedroom with masses of lace and pink stuff her bare body language now left the boys' in no doubt as to what was on offer.

As she disappeared into her bedroom the sight of her undulating ass was probably superfluous to requirements. By this time the two youthful painters and decorators were sporting brittle hard erections. Stevie's was still stretching the fabric of his jeans as his enthusiastic mate, thinking all his Christmases had arrived in one go, flaunted his commendable length and girth. There were no flies on him and off he went in hot pursuit of the lady's ass that had briefly disappeared off the radar screen. By the time he got there Stevie was on the benches so to speak.

Steve had a way with words and he was graphic to say the least. Having appropriately dressed or rather undressed in a manner to fit the occasion he joined the other two in the boudoir and thereupon found himself drawn closer to the amorous couple sexually that was passionately coupling on the nymphet's bed. This was definitely the time for the four-poster to be joined by a fifth column.

By accident or design the two were going at it hammer and tongs and having their fun in the doggie position. Eric, with one hand on the lady's bare shoulder and his other on her hip was exultantly slamming his impressive manhood into her pussy. It was like he was trying to get it into her throat but from the rear entrance.

By this time the stark bollock naked Stevie, also donkey-rigged, is just as closely involved. He is egging the two on and whilst playing with himself he is urging Eric to fucking well hurry up as he wants some of the same. One would have thought that in such a romantic setting Stevie's language would be more loving and tender but as we all know a standing cock has neither conscience nor civility.

At this point, their client sympathetically responded to his fervent impatience. Supporting herself on one hand she took Stevie's manhood, pulled him closer and expertly began to give the lucky lad head. Well, in fact she gave him as much head as he could possibly have prayed for and she was now pumping iron at both ends of her impressive anatomy.

From Eric there soon emerged blasphemous oaths as he experienced his orgasm. It must be said that as it coincided with the lady's deep throat exertions Steve was fortunate or unfortunate enough not to have the met a prematurely similar end. Eric reluctantly withdrew and the lady's amorous clinches. A quick and light sap on Stevie's thigh suggested he take his friend's place. The aroused laddie hardly needed inviting twice. He had of course no idea that his mate had crabs so when he took his turn at giving the lady of the house a good seeing to he was not only fully immersed in her pussy, bathing in his mate's body fluids and taking onboard extra passengers! 'It was my fault then wasn't it?' he asked as plaintively as he held out his hands in despair.

It did not get any better. The subsequent itching became impossible for him to ignore and it was a good time to get some medical input on the unusual and unwanted condition. Again, his friend came to the ill-fated lad's rescue. He offered the advice that bathing the affected regions with strong aftershave would calm the irritation. Then, instead of showing commendable restraint and dabbing a little on to test skin response the hapless lover bathed his genitals copiously in a toxic substance meant for less sensitive parts of the male anatomy. Within seconds of applying the stuff to his penis and testicles poor Steve lit up like a Catherine Wheel. Oh, how he screamed blue murder. Anyone would have thought he had his testicles caught up in his mother's clothes mangle.

Aftershave has an afterlife too. It is not really intended to lose its bite because a little water has been sprinkled on it. It has staying power. It was the desperate need for a little water that then brought Stevie to the sink when following his friend's advice. It rather adds something to the expression, with friends like him why the need for enemies? The water application fell far short of the good intentions behind it. Stevie later said what he should have done in the first place was to do what everyone else did and visit the clap clinic for a cure.

Stevie was what you see on the can or at least what was thought to be in the can before the horsemeat scandal. He was inclined to call a spade a spade and because of his directness he was not too popular with the gentler sex. Shona told of the time when, in a bar, he walked straight up to an attractive woman. Holding her gaze he calmly said, 'I am going to fuck your brains out.'

Not surprisingly he had his ardour cooled by having his pint of lager poured all over him. It was the one time when his directness saved him. Such was his audacious candour that to the lady's boyfriend it suggested he was an escaped inmate from the mental home and he decided to keep his distance.

Whatever one's feelings about Thatcher's British Army it might have been preferable to the life the luckless Stevie was to lead in Leeds. I suppose Gran fondly imagined him to be spending his days working, putting his earnings in a savings account and spending his evenings reading the Greek Oracles. Not so. Soon after arriving in Leeds, he had by chance stumbled upon The Calls. This is the city's Red Light District. Easygoing Stevie soon settled into the community and he would regularly chat up the street girls. He became quite friendly with a few of them and their clients too. One of the girls he met and befriended was a hooker named Chloe. In fact that was her street name but her name was Anna and she was a Bristol girl. She had to leave her home city due to a misunderstanding over a debt owed to some of the city's heavies. Chloe just upped sticks and took off to Leeds. It was a place on the map and the sign on the front of her National Express coach. Why not? Where else?

An attractive girl, Chloe was slim with long fair hair that was not too dissimilar to his own sandy hair. He had befriended her in a bar where it became obvious that before selling herself she needed a few stiffeners of a different kind. Chloe was on methadone and was trying to come clean. She told him she had not used drugs for the past six months. Although not the brightest tool in the box, Steve was not so naïve as to believe her. He had seen it all before.

He was largely indifferent to that side of the situation and in the meantime the two spent time in local bars in their off periods. A popular watering hole for the 'ladies of the night' was the White Swan more commonly known as the Mucky Duck. Due to his unfortunate encounter with the landlady that his Gran had selected for him the wee laddie soon needed to find new digs. Chloe mentioned in passing that there was a spare room going at her flat share.

The engaging newcomer hardly needed to hear her suggestion a second time. This was how he found himself sharing a home with not one but two hookers. It is no surprise that he describes the situation as being the best experience of his life. The two girls, Chloe and Stacy, used the apartment as a place of work so to speak. Steve, ever curious about life's rich tapestry was fascinated by the comings and going and especially the comings. Relaxing in the adjacent room to that where the fun was taking place, and with its lack of soundproofing, he was privy to what was going on in the room used by the girls. The sounds radiating from the room left little for the imagination. In fact he could hear most of the conversation such as it was.

As soon as he heard a punter arrive Steve would find himself becoming as much aroused as was the punter. On hearing the action he was in his imagination either enjoying a threesome or taking the place of the punter. As a consequence to this it was not unusual for Stevie to pleasure himself several times a day. Chloe in her wisdom decided it would be better for their friendship if they kept it platonic but her sentiment was not mutual. Steve thought otherwise and if it were known he constantly fantasised about penetrating his flatmate's most erogenous zones.

Stacy on the other hand didn't care who she screwed. Show her the readies, tell her your tastes and if the price was agreed then any orifice would do including anal. Stacy was not as good looking as was Chloe. According to Steve she was of African descent and unkindly regarded as looking a little like an ape. She had a crown of afro hair as if she had just stepped out of an episode of Starsky and Hutch. Attractive to some, not to others but always a sight to be seen she had a magnificent big duck arse. As a hooker, she dressed for the part and habitually wore her small and tight red PVC skirt. Steve convincingly told us that you could see her snatch without making it too obvious you were looking. Stacy wore the skirt with 'shag me' boots and sure enough looked every inch of the hooker she was. Her lips were like tractor tyres and Steve grinned at the thought that when she gave you a blow job it was the next best thing to a Hoover vacuum cleaner. He had tried that?

Stacy had previously lived with her strait-laced parents in the city's Chapeltown district. Up until a year earlier had been attending church with her family. Stevie's flatmate had rebelled against her ultra respectable claustrophobic home life and allowed herself to be courted and influenced by a boyfriend who was in fact a pimp.

The charmer was a smooth talker and he flattered her so much that she had fallen for him hook line and sinker. Little did she realise that she was being soft talked into accepting into a life of prostitution. He had convinced her that taking a relaxed attitude towards sex with others, provided that it was a purely physical and financially lucrative calling, wasn't as bad as it has been made out to be. That it was often mutually enjoyable, that she was getting paid for being laid. It did not mean she could not reserve real heart love for her seducer.

She had not so much chosen the path but had been levered into it through grooming and at times a little blackmail and arm-twisting. Having led a sheltered life she was an innocent dupe and too naive to comprehend that she was being deliberately being made drug dependent. This was the callous intention of her boyfriend. He had no interest in her as a person and nor did he have any interest in her in a romantic sense. To him she was simply a woman who could fuck on an industrial scale and all he could see were the dollar signs. It was better than owning a shop and making a living from it. The overheads were fewer and there was less hassle once 'the business' had been set up. He was confident that Stacy would soon be one of his bitches. Adept at doing what he did best he was soon to be proved right.

On one occasion he had beaten her up so badly that she had been hospitalised. Stacy's transgression - she had a target to meet and she had failed to meet it. Although she was in a bad way she never talked to the cops and she refused to grass her pimp. He turned up at the hospital and it was agreed that she kept her thoughts and her experience to herself and in return he would not attack her again. That was chivalrous of him. Fortunately for Chloe's flatmate he kept his word. It was most likely because a badly beaten up hooker is less likely to appeal to potential clients.

We were totally taken aback at Steve's revelations. We had hardly led a sheltered lifestyle but his world was so much different from ours. The youngster, for he still was a young man, explained in that matter of fact way of his that he wouldn't touch Stacy's (arse) with a copper's erection. This was taken to mean that he was partial to Stacy giving him head but whatever was between her meaty thighs was off limits. She was generous with it. It was an offering of hers that was offered bareback and that was a risk too far in his opinion. Shagging Stacy was not worth catching a bug but the girl had no shortage of punters, many of whom returned time after time.

Chapter 14
The gathering

Different strokes for different folks. Stevie because of the cremation found himself back in Glasgow on a one-way ticket. Whilst he loved his home city he found it difficult to come to terms with the reason for his being there and was obliged to just accept things. Following the service at Deborah's funeral, which likely reminded him of his own mortality; Stevie became very subdued and had little to say for himself. Shona sensed the change of mood and suggested they should all head for the local bar. The cremation had taken place in Castlemilk and is hardly the most inviting of places to find oneself in. It is if anything a bit of a dive despite the beautiful landscaped cemetery.

When asking a local where they might find a decent pub it was suggested that they head for The Brown Cow. They explored but couldn't find a pub with such a name but they did find one named The Shirley Bassey. Ordering the round they enquired as to the whereabouts of the Shirley Bassey pub and were told they were told they were in it. The Brown Cow was the name given to the Shirley Bassey by disrespectful locals.

The Shirley Bassey was a soulless bar. Any effort to make it welcoming had been abandoned a long time ago as a lost cause. The only contribution to happiness was the 'happy hour'. The drinks were on reduced price. It was not a lot to cheer the small group of mourners up but they were philosophical as always about their lot.

The core of the more optimistic members of the group; along with their spokesman Shona, tried to liven the mood and salvage something of the depressing day.

Maddie and Alfie who needed a lift with a stronger kick than that provided by alcohol spent no time at all in heading for the toilets. It wasn't long before they were in their own private heavens. It was their way of dealing with things and all agreed that a good night ahead was just what was needed. An effort was made to brighten the mood and songs broke out - there was an enforced frivolity so essential to their upcoming parting and their going there separate ways.

The bar-cum-restaurant was one of those rooms with a smoking and no smoking section. Smokers and non-smokers we were all smokers passive or otherwise. As a friend remarked, having a smoking only section was a bit like having a pissing only section of the municipal swimming pool.

The bar prices at the Shirley Bassey were at least reasonable. Every cloud has a silver lining. As soon as the drinks appeared the room's tables were jerked together by the men in the group and it was bottoms up for the great lyricist, Robbie Burns. As we settled down to our drinks Maddie was notably absent. 'It's a bit strange,' I remarked to Shona.

Just as we were preparing ourselves to go and look for her my sister reappears with the notorious twin cousins Justin and Joey on each of her arms. Where on earth had she found them? We were totally taken aback. Had we been in the area frequented by the pair of thugs it wouldn't have been a big deal but here they were taking their chances. Because they were off their patch and undoubtedly on someone else's there was no personal safety here, not even in numbers. Certainly not for the kind of local gangsters who might have the twins in their crosshairs and quite possibly so with much justification.

I felt an involuntary shiver as the twin, Justin and Joey glanced around the group. Whenever I looked at the two I shivered and I wondered what it must be like for their victims. The smart suited gangsters' eyes momentarily met mine and I could not help but notice that the pupils of their eyes were like pinheads. Their weird mannerisms and appearance suggested they were high on something. They are what happens in a lawless society where life is as cheap as the next fix. The two expressed their condolences whilst adding that their presence was due to the respect they had for my father. They explained that it would have been disrespectful to have actually attended the service itself. What did they know about respect other than the term in their own perverted sense of it? What respect did their victims ever receive from them?

Shona, who initially felt uneasy with the twins, remembered the time that they got Deborah out deep shit at the party and remarked that since then they had mellowed. She still had an unavoidable sense of foreboding but she was prepared to get on with them at face value.

Hardly surprisingly Stevie was now in much better spirits. He had salvaged something of his innate sense of humour and was now set upon being the life and soul of the party. This was to be Stevie's first encounter with the twins and they got on famously. He cheerfully relived some of his earlier Leeds stories for the twins benefit. It appeared it would be a night of nostalgia sharing reminisces of his experiences with prostitutes. As the chat continued we learnt that Justin and Joey had acquired shares in a strip joint and keeping an eye on their investment was keeping the two occupied. We all knew what that meant.

We hadn't seen either of the twins since Deborah had left the Gorbals. Maddie was often to be found there but even she hadn't encountered the twins. It now appeared that they had a new venture in the Milk or Baby Land as it was known as. This was because of the numbers of young single mums being housed there. They were hardly more than schoolgirls but would soon be taking their offspring to the schools they had so recently left.

Shona when chatting to Justin and Joey showed her curiosity by asking if there had been any dramas in their lives of late. Thinking about it later I thought this was a pretty dumb question to ask these two mobsters. Wherever they were there was likely to be drama. For God's sake they were drama. They were amiable enough and they laughed together at her question. They then began to tell a story about a friend of theirs. This particular drama had unfolded at a strip bar called Teasers so no subtlety there then.

As it turned out the friend they were commenting on was none other but Mark aka known as Stanley as in DIY knife. It seemed that the luckless lad was out of his brains due to whatever he was using. At this point he was getting over familiar with the club's strippers. This is precisely the sort of behaviour that upsets the bouncers. They warned Stanley that his behaviour was out of order and he was courteously invited to vacate the premises. It mattered not that the twins were his bosom buddies. He had transgressed and club rules were rules. The girls were sacrosanct unless a punter had an arrangement. Stanley of course did not.

Stanley was at the time coked up and had been sniffing Amyl Nitrate. Whatever, he wasn't that much out of it that he didn't perceive the upcoming threat as the bouncers homed in on him like Scud missiles. In his wide-eyed panic and desperation to avoid their physical attention, much of his popper bottle's contents splashed over him. It wasn't a good time to learn that poppers, being solvent based, are highly inflammable when they come into contact with any fluid.

All hell went loose as the disastrous Stanley set fire to himself. Justin's mind had gone into fast-forward and grabbing a nearby fire extinguisher he hit the nozzle. Fear turned quickly to fun as Stanley was given a good hosing down. He sure knew how a car feels when it goes through the car wash. Stanley just stood there speechless and looking for all the world like a foamy snowman. His expression said it all. 'What the fuck! Did that shit just happen?'

Stanley wisely thought that when you're in a hole you stop digging and he decided to call it a night. Tidying himself up but failing abysmally he called a cab and slunk home with his tail between his legs. Every cloud has a silver lining we surmised. Was there ever a better time for his giving up smoking?

Justin had us holding our bellies and screeching as he recounted the tale. Someone mentioned Stanley shrieking like a banshee and that set us all off again. Maddie reminded us about the solemnity of the occasion but I did little to dampen the good humour. There was no question about it. Although the twins had an annoying arrogance to go with their swagger the pair was truly charismatic. Introductions to other members of the family were amusing. I don't think the brothers quite got their head around the fact that we were all family as it was something of an extended family. The blood running through their veins was all the same.

It was soon clear to Shona that the brothers had taken a shine to Trina. As people were chatting among themselves in little groups or couples Shona and I moved around. We wanted everyone to feel they were part of the bigger picture. Our eyes rolled when we saw Justin and his brother smooth talking Trina. For God's sake she is family and kissing cousins is taboo.

It might have been acceptable if kissing was all the two had in mind but whilst others had a policy of not kissing on a first date these two expected the full Monty on their first date. No doubt they were also considering the prospect of Trina servicing their special clientele'. Whatever else might be said of Trina and her morals or lack of them, she was a hooker and she was a looker too. There was a bonus in that she didn't yet have the gaunt and haunted look associated with junkies. That's yet to come and she kept her youthful looks. Justin and Joey knew she was on the game and her naturally curvaceous figure added up to a nice bank balance in their eyes.

Trina, when chatting, told me that when she had briefly lived in the Gorbals for no more than a short while she had been introduced to Justin and Joey. She didn't of course know they were related and there was no reason for her to think so. Maddie still hadn't forgiven Trina for the occasion when, released from the rehab centre she had been bawling up at her window and wanting to know if she had any kit. For this reason she referred to Trina as Trashy Trina.

Mother was less than impressed at Trina's coarseness and she wasted no time at all in recounting the tale to her sister Katie. What Trina overlooked mentioning was that she had actually had a one to one encounter with the brothers. To put a fine point on it she had found herself to be the meat in their sandwich. Whatever floats your boat and we were to later discover that threesomes were normal for Justin and Joey. It is nice when siblings share but on that occasion the pair took things far beyond convention.

In all fairness there was no shortage of girls who were attracted to the bad boys of the community. In this respect the Gorbals was no different from anywhere else. Trina found herself seduced by their double-barrelled charm. She had a similar effect on their hearts and other parts of their anatomy too. Being streetwise Trina was no one's fool and was under no illusions about their expectations of her. They hardly needed to spell it out and whatever she imagined their needs to be they coincided with her thoughts. To her it was opportunity with security. With Trina there wasn't much that wasn't on the table of sexual activity. This included sex in a threesome with her cousins.

To give Trina her due she found little need to be overly graphic as to the events that weekend. Putting things as delicately as she could, we just knew they started proceedings by the sniffing of coke. Well, if you're going to do something you might as well get the most out of it and it seems to have added a little more lead in their pencils. Encouraged by the flexible and equally naked Trina the night was spent by the twins doing to her whatever turned them on. The twins were very demanding of her. Trina was equally accommodating. Reading between the lines it had all been as depraved as it gets. Anything one can do two can do and that is precisely what they did and in every orifice. Some live for debasement. Joey, Justin and Trina revelled in self-debasement.

If the twins had ulterior motives then she had her own too. There was going to be a bill at the end of that weekend's freebie. She knew well enough the importance of discretion and was streetwise enough to screw not only their manhood's but whatever else they could give her to make ends meet. What wasn't speculative was that Trina was as depraved as the twins were and she got as much out of the encounter as they did. She also got a job out of it as her CV came up very good that steamy weekend.

It was not a situation where cash changed hands but the boys did give her a little something by way of a job at one of their brothels. Even if the wily Trina had not been certain if the nights' of unbridled sex was an interview she soon learnt that she had passed with flying colours. By all accounts it was a mutually agreeable understanding. We did know that Trina was in a bad way when she was living in the Gorbals. What we didn't know, mostly because we were not that interested, was that she could hardly have descended morally lower. By that time she had only her body to barter.

There was no doubt about it Trina was a much changed person. She never got over being gratuitously raped when strapped to the radiator as a consequence of her partner's unpaid bill. From there on the norms of morality and convention eluded her. The rape had put her outside the comforting restraints of conformity. To drop to the same degrading level as her attackers was her psychological way of dealing with it. To this day she has flashbacks through which she relives the pain and humiliation. We could understand her feelings.

Trina had got herself back on her feet if you went by her appearance. No one could question her overall good looks, her grooming, deportment and her vibrant personality. Not surprisingly men were attracted to her and the attention she received from the twins was par for the course. It was a foregone conclusion that they would click and none perhaps knew or cared that they were related. There was unlikely to be progeny from any couplings anyway. Would she care had she known? Possibly not for she had reached the stage where any sex outside the norm was within her remit. Someone remarked that she would have closed her eyes and thought of her next fix if her pappy had wanted her in his bed.

Under no illusions we knew what she was capable of doing. She had been caught on camera cashing other people's giros and their Monday books. The courts never sent her down. She received small fines and to compensate for each financial loss she stole some more. The court fines were actually fuelling her stealing exploits. Ironically, the court's clerk who took her fines might easily have been prosecuted for receiving and laundering stolen monies.

Was she given an opportunity to straighten herself out at the rehabilitation centre? No, they just upped her social security allowance as her drug problem was taken into consideration. So there we have it: The authorities in their wisdom or lack of it reward drug users. Welcome to Scotland! Welcome to Absurdistan.

Deborah's wake at the Brown Cow pub was more than a meeting of the minds; it was a crossroads watering hole for some. It certainly was for Trina. Soon after the funeral and related events she would be back on the heroin. She would also go back on the game and in time her daughter would be taken from her care by the child's father. Trina was at the top of a very slippery slope and the party that day sort of gave her a push in the back to get her re-started. The family were fast running out of patience with her. She was increasingly ostracised but given the girl's unfortunate background and experience it has been asked if understanding and support might have led to a far better outcome. In this case then consciences would be clearer than they now are.

It was getting quite late now and I was physically and mentally drained. I was desperate for the day to end but Alfie and Maddie; in fact Shona too, had other plans. They had by now enthusiastically scampered on to the dance floor and were treadin' the light fantastic. I had enough of all that and not long afterwards my seat was empty. As it turned out, my leaving was to be a blessing in disguise. I was to hear that a brawl had soon afterwards broken out and as usual it was over something quite trivial. All it needed was the smallest spark. A wrong expression, a misinterpretation, something minor, that could be perceived as an over familiarity. It didn't have to be much to start a fist-swinging altercation. That may be the case but it doesn't have to be a huge issue to throw people into life changing or life stopping situations.

Stevie isn't alone in having a fondness for beer and he is hardly unique in being a bit loud when the booze is doing the talking. It doesn't usually get a hostile reaction. He is obviously a crack-head on the booze and tolerance is shown towards him. 'He doesn't mean any harm.' The dance section of the floor that night had been heaving. The bar, having an extended licence meant that most people were either drunk, on a drug-fuelled high or most probably both. It was an atmosphere that could turn toxic and it was only waiting for someone to touch the blue touch paper. This happened when Stevie accidentally banged into an arse hole at the bar. This caused friction and poor Stevie found himself kissing this guy's bottle of Grolsch. He was lucky the blow never took his eye out wonky or not.

The happier atmosphere instantly morphed into a poisonous one. The girls screamed, presumptions were made and the next thing there was a free for all that would have done justice to a barroom fight in a Western movie. Justin and Joey thought it was a cabaret and they got wired too. They weren't waiting for an invitation, the more sensible minded headed straight for the doors. For Shona a quick exit was not possible as there were now more bottles flying through the air than shells and shrapnel at Ypres. Fixated and scared for herself poor Shona flung herself under a table and cowered trembling.

The evening events ended with a high casualty list including the walking wounded. Ironically Stevie wasn't the one to come worst off. The twins had shown their true colours and both were gratuitously vicious as one might expect. There were a few in attendance that would leave with scars that would be carried with them to their graves.

Teddy was a tough guy and having taken to the brothers he got stuck into the melee. He was inspired by the sight of his cousin getting glassed or rather by the spouting red claret that resulted from the underhanded blow. Despite his toughness Teddy doesn't usually get caught up in a fracas but he had taken this affront personally. Blood is blood and never more so than when it is spilled.

Teddy would tell me later his version of events and despite the cosmetics it didn't get any better. He said he was quietly stood at the bar having just ordered his round. It was then that he heard Stevie cussing and cursing. His curiosity having got the better of him he recognised

Stevie's voice and he then took himself off to investigate. It must have been a sight to behold, especially for the more mild mannered and better behaved locals. There was a loud mouthed Cockney in the company of a Glaswegian whose accent you could cut with a knife up against a Glasgow horde. It was supposed it wouldn't be obvious they were all family but they soon cottoned on.

Teddy did not emerge unscathed. His ribs ached painfully and he had a shiner and a lip that looked like a car tyre inner tube. Other than that only his pride had taken a hammering. To my knowledge most of the family weren't in the habit of being tooled up but in this respect neither Justin nor Joey could be presumed to be without back up. As Shona was reliving the night's events my first thoughts were for Alfie and Maddie. Fortunately their night had started early and having passed out they remained oblivious of the entire shambles and later could recall only the aftermath.

My father was all ears when hearing of what had occurred at Deborah's wake. When he heard that the twins were involved on the very night of Deborah's cremation he was filled with disgust. His one consolation was that the brothers had not been invited but had chanced upon the occasion. Shona stood up for the pair by pointing out that the finger of blame should really be pointed at Stevie. The truth was it had been a minor upset blown up out of proportion and for what outcome? Mother was unaware of the event as still under doctor's orders she was heavily sedated and there was still a little way to go before she would return to her normal self. Only then would the clan be summoned so that she might hear their version of events.

There were several consequences of that brawl and

the truth was unpalatable. Within a day or two the uniforms arrived at my mother's home and didn't exactly receive a 21 gun salute. Throughout my life there had been a heavy police presence. They were helpful sometimes and there were times when they could be arrogant arseholes. Nonetheless, whichever of these categories they fitted into they were not welcome in my mother's house.

Mother knew Sergeant Andrews and willingly shook his hand. Not so his 'invisible' female colleague who kept her protective gear on and appeared to be aloof. Sergeant Andrews was no stranger to our family and its passage through life. True, he had been involved in some of the dawn raids on our home but nevertheless he came across as a good and sympathetic man. He seemed to know that he was not upholding civil order, he was papering over the cracks where it failed. On this occasion he was genuinely sympathetic in offering his condolences for the death of my sister, Deborah. As far as you could trust a 'turncoat', mother had faith in him. The sergeant was not one of us and he never would be, but he was treated with less caution than were his less trustworthy uniformed colleagues. My mother had not forgotten how he had given Deborah a break on occasion. Sergeant Andrews could have had my younger sister up for the breach on numerous occasions. He was too kindly to do so and gave her a caution instead. Deborah was known to the police and many had a soft spot for her. Deborah was not bad as in wicked. My sister had spent a fair few nights in the local constabulary's cells and she had never been treated with other than civility. The kindly gestures offered by PC Plod were appreciated.

There you are then, Mother was asked on this occasion what did she know about who was in a certain bar. Mother of course was completely clueless. She was so innocent and out of it that she thought it possible that the visit was some kind of stunt based on a candid camera television show. In a word she had no idea what the police sergeant was talking about. Needless to say it wasn't long before the visiting rozzers put some detail to the purpose of their call.

Alfie had been named as being present at the fracas. This was despite the fact that he never frequented Castlemilk. Would anyone, given an alternative choice? Alfie too had served time in prison and to cap it all he had been witnessed by some from Longriggend Prisons. Alfie had pissed a few folk off in his time and maybe now it was payback. Whatever was behind his being fingered he was grassed. It then occurred to me to question how come, amidst of this chaos at the club, the cops never showed up until the bar was practically empty.

We heard through the grapevine the general consensus was who was going to name names and what the remaining bar clientele saw. Everyone questioned was vague because the fracas had erupted to quickly in an already confusing situation. The police did not pressure any whom they questioned. They knew that what had gone on was no gang fight. It was just another bar brawl. All that was left for the onlookers to do was to make certain the seriously injured: those who were unable to flee were attended to. Apparently, in amongst the chaos there was heard a shrieking siren that forewarned everyone that the rozzers were on their way. When that happens no one wants to be caught injured or carrying someone who is.

A bunch of girlie guys found hiding in the ladies and two other guys were ambulated out. No-one knows or claims to know who the fucker was that stuck the Phillips screwdriver in his cheek and had nearly completely mutilated his face by trying his best to retrieve it. The sick fucker wanted it back so he could do it all over again. The devil truly walked amongst us.

Maniacs were apparently lurking under the bar's shadows. Nobody could possibly have foreseen such an outcome. The police were quite detailed in the description of the aforementioned. As they rambled on they were largely talking to themselves as Mother was out of the loop. Madeline and Shona were called in the presence of my father and were instructed to tell the officers what they knew of the incident. Quick-thinking Shona told them they should do their job and check the CCTV records. Many bars back then would have as deterrent, dummy cameras and these at times like this were as useless as a bull with tits. People just assumed the cameras were operating as they should.

The evidence so far collated was speculative; it was word of mouth and hearsay and gave mother no cause for alarm or concern. She was pretty cool and anyway sedated to her eyeballs. The rozzers exited no wiser than when they had arrived. Mission not accomplished. Mother had thought they were there to pay their respects and express their regrets over the death of Deborah. It wouldn't be the first time that the boys in blue would come to my mother's door to tell her that they were looking for Alfie. On each occasion she had irksomely and venomously slammed the door and told them in an interesting choice of words that he was in Longriggend Prison He likely was.

On the occasion of this visit by the uniforms we each knew exactly where Alfie was. He was up in his bedroom sleeping the previous night's excesses off. Mother might well have pretended he was otherwise incommunicado as there was no way, if questioned; they were going to get any sense out of him anyway. She had on the hour popped up to see him and made sure that he had not been sick and she tilted his head to the side to made sure he could breathe uninterrupted. She knew he was in a bad way and she was determined she would not lose another of her children. Mother told the officers in her own sweet way to do one. They informed both Maddie and Shona that they should make themselves available for questioning. That was the least of their worries. Not long afterwards I took the call from Teddy who was at the hospital. Stevie was in theatre and surgeons were frantically trying to save his eye.

It was a bad time no doubt but in a converse way the situation made us focus on something other than our sister and for that we were all grateful. All of the injured parties in our family fared pretty well as opposed to their contenders. It could have been much worse and we could easily have been buying a family member in addition to poor Deborah. . God most definitely works in mysterious ways and for that we no doubt privately all bowed our heads and prayed a sincere thank you.

Chapter 15
Shona´s story

One day a whole chapter of bikers entered the bar and one of the guys immediately caught Shona's attention. My sister had a preference for tall men and at 6 foot and 5 inches he was difficult to miss even in a crowded bar. Shona said later that he had really girly eye lashes as if he wore mascara. They were just naturally long and when I eventually met him I knew just what she meant. He introduced himself to her as Terry as he ordered a round in for his five mates. Terry told her he was working as a courier. He laughed as he told Shona that courier's had a very short life expectancy in London. In this case, he added, he might as well enjoy himself. Shona agreed that he had a valid point as couriering in London was a dangerous job. He went on to tell Shona, who said that at the point she was all ears. He pointed out to her two guys on the fruit machine and told her that unfortunately they were his brothers.

The pair smiled and introduced themselves as Morris aka Tex and Vinny. Like their brother Terry they were big lads too. As a British Army serviceman Tex had just finished his tour of duty in Northern Ireland. This was the reason they were out celebrating. The two other guys in the group were couriers also but they were dwarfed by these three big geezers. One went by the name of Jason and he was tiny at just 5' 2" and the other, Les, who was Vinny's mate were both Taekwondo instructors. Shona had no qualms in conceding that she didn't know what he was talking about and so he good naturedly explained that it was a form of martial arts.

Taekwondo combines combat and self defence techniques with sport and exercise. Shona looked up at him and wondered why he would need self-defence lessons. After all, he was built like a brick shithouse and was very self-disciplined in his habits. He didn't drink alcohol and he was totally anti smoking. My dear sister said she felt like she was in Lilliput being surrounded by giants. There was only the one who could talk face to face without their having to bend down.

That Friday night in the Drake pub it was starting to get busy. Shona never had much of an opportunity to speak to Terry but I could tell during our phone conversation that there was something about him that she instantly liked. She took on as many shifts at the Drake Pub as she could now that she had stopped temping. My sister had little choice as she was short of money. There was a big difference in her finances now as bar work didn't pay as well as did her temping jobs. Sure, she knew she needed a break and she was really enjoying it.

Sunday would normally have been a day that Shona would not be at work. Very often, on a Saturday night, after the bar had closed its doors, someone was holding a party somewhere and invariably the bar staff were invited. Shona liked to recuperate and enjoy a long lie-in on a Sunday and she had by tradition committed herself to Sunday lunch with Aunt Bella. On a whim that day she popped into the bar to pick up her rota for the following week, it was spontaneous choice normally she would phone for her hours. When she arrived, Terry and his two brothers were gathered around the pool table, they were clearly enjoying themselves. Shona said her eyes lit up when she saw Terry and added that she felt all goose pimply like a silly school kid. Whilst waiting for Tracey to bring Sean with her next week's rota; Shona perched on a bar stool. Spotting his opportunity, Terry approached her and offered to buy Shona a drink. She accepted of course and she asked for her favourite tipple. In the meantime Sean gave her have the following week's rota, after which she began chatting to Terry. Shona could tell that he was flirting with her and she was upbeat about it afterall she was playing the same game with him.

After he asked her if she could play pool and she had told him yes, my sister spent the rest of the afternoon with Terry. Sadly, for Aunt Bella, the traditional lunch fell by the wayside. The relationship having got off to a good start ended in their being a couple. We all thought how wonderful, a 'marriage' made in heaven. How wrong could we be? At the beginning of their relationship Shona was flattered that he would go out of his way to be with her. He was constantly calling in at the bar where she worked. She thought of it as showing his caring nature. She was too blind to see it for what it was; Terry was a control freak. For Shona it was her first time in love but it would not take her too long to see what was really happening right under her eyes. Personally, I think even a short time is too long when it comes to the penny dropping. We voiced our concerns but Shona had cloth ears. No one's as blind as those who will not see.

Of course these things don't just happen overnight but they creep in very slowly. I was the first to notice that Shona didn't call in as much. I knew she was working long hours and I would try to call but found it almost impossible to catch her in. We didn't know that when Terry was at Shona's flat he would unplug the phone. This strange habit of his went unnoticed for a long time but it was put down to someone having tugged too hard at the cord. After it happened time and time again the girls suggested that someone was doing it on purpose. Terry, for my liking, was too good to be true. With film star appeal and good looks he was too mushy and too full of himself. I knew that Shona was definitely smitten when she told me on the phone that the night before she had lost her virginity. Terry had been 'so loving' towards her that the experience was quite magical, sick bags all round I thought. Still, it was her business and she was an adult so she knew what she was doing. Terry seemed to work less and less as a courier and was soon spending more and more time with Shona.

This honeymoon period was beginning to stifle Shona a bit, she liked her space; Terry didn't appreciate that at all when she told him. She said she wanted to spend a bit more time with her girlfriends. At first he seemed to take this suggestion in good spirits. He stopped phoning Shona and he then stopped coming to the bar. For about a week he seemed to have just dropped off the face of the earth. Shona was too inexperienced to realise that this was just a ploy to make her feel guilty and for her to do all the running.

His ploy worked like a dream. Shona made the first move, apologised and young love was all back on again. They both agreed that they would spend more time with their friends but in reality it never happened. Whenever Shona was out with friends he would be passing by, or would just turn up, it was to the point that it was very embarrassing for Shona and she would make excuses for him. On a few occasions she found him looking through her handbag and one day caught him checking up on her dental appointments. The penny dropped. He had been going through her personal things and Shona knew this lack of trust was not heading to a good place.

Shona was however thrilled that Sean had given her an opportunity to strike out on her own. She wasted no time at all in bidding Bella adieu and thanking her profusely for all her support and help. Aunt Bella said, 'it was my pleasure.' You are family you have been like a daughter to me. Shona knew how much Bella would miss her and she made a point of mentally noting that she would keep in touch on a regular basis. Shona kept true to her word.

Sean had saved her a lot of hassle in finding her shared accommodation and the owner didn't want a couple of months rent as a deposit. For that she was eternally grateful. Shona had only been working at the bar for about six weeks and she said the staff and the regulars were a great crack. My lovely sister explained to me that Sean and his girlfriend Anya ran the bar but it was Sean who owned the bar.

The Irishman had arrived in London about ten years earlier and had been a builder in his previous calling. He had no desire to leave his homeland but like so many others had been obliged to leave in search of a better life. He and Shona were under no illusions. Both knew that there weren't many opportunities in Scotland or Ireland. There really was not a whole heap of options. Sean was very ambitious and was in not in the slightest work-shy.

Shona said he thought he was God's gift and considered himself to be an Irish Adonis. Shona also thought that he was one of those dudes who clearly worked out and at every opportunity. Sean wore a white tight vest to complement his six-pack. His smile was such that he was like a walking advert for a dentist, amazing that he too, like Terry, was like something out of

Hollywood. She added that as is the case with many Irish folks Sean had a fantastic sense of humour which went down a storm. He was the best publican one could imagine. Certainly he had kissed a few Blarneys in his time. After a few years of applying graft and charm he would achieve his dream and set his eyes on his own home. He knew also that his father would be so proud of his success.

The engaging barman had met his girlfriend Anya when she had ventured into the bar on a drunken hen night. All the girls that night were dressed as Playboy bunnies and they were all certainly the worst for wear. Anya caught his eye and he was smitten and she had him hooked. From there on he decided that she would be his trophy and that was that; it was settled. Two days after their first meeting that had occurred a year earlier she had moved her things upstairs to his apartment.

Apart from Shona there were three other members of staff. At the weekends my sister worked with Angie and Tracey. On several occasions Shona told me that she did not like her colleagues. There was something about them that she did not trust. The two made no secret that they were dykes and they both had a bit of attitude. Shona later would tell me that at first she found them to be very intimidating. She said they were huge but in Shona's case such a statement meant only that they were over five foot four inches. She added that they wore their ribbons on their sleeves and were out loud and proud gays. Of course, there in your face lesbianism wouldn't normally have been tolerated behind a bar but Sean turned his eye and the Irishman revelled in their passing gropes.

He had originally suggested that the girls wear matching skin-tight shamrock t-shirts shirts. His partner Anya put her foot down and said it would be like the

American Hooters and she added darkly that it would lower the tone of the bar. The bar owner teased her and reminded her that the first night they had met she was dressed as a playboy bunny and holding a dildo in her mouth. Anyway, the t-shirt idea never happened which was probably just as well. Carmen was the remaining member of their team and she was from the Caribbean. Like other West Indians she arrived in London and was keen to better herself and to give her kids a better life. Thirty years on and what had she done with her life? She was cleaning somebody's crap out of the toilets. Still she was proud her children were doing well and that was all she wished for.

Sean thoughtfully helped Shona move from Aunt Bella's to her new apartment. The move itself was no biggie. Apart from clothes and a hair dryer she really had no other material possessions. That would be how Shona would live throughout her years in London. Her travelling companions were black bin liners. My sister epitomised the term back to basics. Her boss had never actually lived in the same premises as it was just one of the many investments the bar owner had made. He was an absolute property bore, whose mantra was, location, location, location. While this was being rammed down our throats and ears the television daytime programmes were popping up every time you turned on. The department store sheds like B & Q must have been coining from the constant home improvement campaign being conducted by the television media.

Shona was sardonic and her cheeky riposte was to one night wear a t-shirt carrying the words, 'I don't give a shit how much your house is worth.' She had decided she was she was so sick of it all. Everywhere you went all people spoke about was how much value had been lobbed on their home that week. It was not a home anymore, it was an investment. It was not the usual sentiments that encourage home ownership but it was thoughtless greed. Thank you Mrs Thatcher for that little gem! I think Shona made her point with the t-shirt. Her new flat mates, Kirsty and Rebecca where not exactly unknown to Shona. She had met them on several occasions since she had started working evenings at the bar. There had been the usual exchanged pleasantries and then Shona resumed her wench-like position. She got on with serving and everyone was a happy bunny.

That was that until now. Shona didn't realise that before she had agreed to take the room the girls had taken a vote on whether they thought her suitable. The vote went in Shona's favour if that is the right word in this context. The other girl tenants voted that she seemed nice enough to share with three single white females in London. The house was beautiful despite it being a rather dilapidated Victorian house in need of a little tender loving care. Their home was split into two levels with the girls on top and two biker guys below - in a manner of speaking. The guys were in what might better be described as the basement area. The flat itself was quite spacious. Shona's bedroom was a roomy double sized area and in need of a decent lick of paint. No problem with that. The other bedrooms were pretty much on a par in terms of size and decoration, soft furnishings and views from the windows. The shared kitchen area had been newly decorated and had named cupboards. As Shona was describing all this on the telephone to me one Saturday evening I was in hysterics. Named cupboards, for goodness sake! I had never heard the likes. I knew that one day it would not make for a happy ending and I told Shona as much. I would be later proved right.

Shona was clearly excited about the new direction her life was taking and further explained that the house overlooked a lovely little green area with a few strategically positioned benches dotted around. Each had a shiny brass plaque sponsored by someone or other. Furthermore, the house was not too far from the train station. That was a bonus. In London you need to rely on Shank's Pony or on public transport. Cycling in London is only an option for the brain dead and the stupid. Shona would have to tighten her belt and throw in some overtime to adapt to her new home and lifestyle. Until now she had not acted prudently and her money management skills were zilch. It wasn't helped because previously she had enjoyed surplus cash; she had boarded with Aunt Bella, rent free: Everything, outside of her aunt's had a price tag, especially independence.

Shona instantly took a shine to the two girls she was sharing with, particularly Rebecca. Maybe they clicked because of their lineage and Celtic connection. Becks as she preferred to be called, was originally from Dublin. Rebecca was a gentle creature. The Irish girl wasn't loud or an in your face type. She also had a Celtic / Mediterranean look about her not too dissimilar in appearance to Shona. Same olive-type complexion and similarly she was brown-eyed. However, unlike Shona she was not quite as diminutive and at 5' 7' was I suppose average. A nice looking girl, most blokes when chatting with Becks had difficulty keeping their focus on her face. Her breasts were generously sized and beautifully shaped and so she could easily have become a tabloid page three girl.

As did my sister, Rebecca had had the contents of the Holy Bible rammed down her throat for years but was philosophical about her background. Her attitude was, why the fuck should I care about getting burnt in the inferno? What will be, will be anyway? She was very laid back and like her fellow flat mates she liked nothing better than dossing, chilling and having a smoke. In truth she was a total smack-head. Becks was doing a little research work for a friend of hers but kept her cards very close to her chest and did not elaborate on the type of work she was engaged in. Shona and Kirsty were naturally curious about her and what she did for a living but no matter how much they quizzed their friend she never divulged. We would later learn that Becks was a kept lady. As far as we were concerned she was lucky as most days it meant she could work from home. She would just log on, get stoned and then channel hop.

Rebecca had come a long way from her humble beginnings. Her coming to the smoke had been an act of faith. As had many other Irish girls and boys she quickly adapted to city life. Beck's big ambition was to get rich quick whatever it took and then she would then be free to be the slob she always wanted to be. She aspired to being a lady who did lunch.

Kirsty on the other hand was proud as Punch of being an Essex girl and she loved her stereotypical white stilettos. I guess she just played to the crowd and she loved the attention she received. Like Becks, Kirsty had been blessed with good looks. Unlike her flatmates she had blonde hair. Okay, she had a little help from the bottle but she still looked scrumptious. Kirsty was also blessed with amazing deep blue sea eyes curtained by long natural eye lashes. Had she been a tad lighter in weight she would have been a real knock-out. Unlike Rebecca, Kirsty was loud.

She wasn't originally from the region of white stilettos but was from England's North-East, Newcastle. Kirsty had been an eight year old child when her parents divorced and with her mother she had relocated to Essex. She told my sister that she hated Essex so much at first that she hitched all the way back to Geordie land in the hope she could live with her father. That was not going to happen. He had other plans and had, by then, a new family. It was made perfectly clear to her that she was not welcome. Turned around Kirsty was then escorted back to Essex courtesy of the police. Since that humiliating rejection she had not spoken to her father or been in contact with her half siblings. Kirsty was disinterested and evidently the sentiment was reciprocated. The youngster was without a doubt loud and had a very heavy Essex accent with a little Geordie twang thrown in. Shona says on more than one occasion she would have to say, 'Wow slowdown, what the fuck?' and ask her to repeat herself. Shona was also asked on many occasions to repeat herself when she was chatting. She modified it and we would tease her new posh voice.

Shona retaliated with retorts such as you have to speak slowly or nobody would have a Scooby what you were on about. Later in life my sister would be one of the slowest talking Glaswegians you would ever meet and was incredibly accentuated. However, Kirsty could come across as brazen. If it was quiet in her room she was either sleeping or she was out somewhere. The blonde from Essex was brash and not really Shona's cup of tea at all. It was compensated for by her being up for a laugh. She over compensated for her father's rejection by her behaviour and couldn't hold onto a relationship if she tried. She always managed, seemingly on purpose, to screw things up. Kirsty could be quite a self destructive person and drank daily. Shona's flatmate was also heavily dependent upon ganja and in common with her flatmates loved to just chill. As a character Kirsty was unique.

The girl had just started a new job working in a call centre chatting to punters on a sex line and said happily to us avid listeners that the money for old rope. On many occasions, whilst on the telephone to Shona, I would hear Kirsty in the background laughing loudly. I thought to myself, 'OMG! This is a blast. I wish I could be there eavesdropping with Shona. Kirsty told Shona that she had been working as a temp but she had been caught in a compromising situation with her boss. As a consequence she was invited to clear her desk and not slam the door on the way out. That was hardly surprising; the employee who had caught the pair fucking each other was none other than the cheating husband's wife. She wasn't then likely to be the only one to be told to clear the desk.

Kirsty said that the pair were going at it like hammer and tongs. They were on the office floor with her on top of the woman's husband and with her bare arse in full view. She was riding the guy's erection like a rodeo rider when the door slammed open. Kirsty said she got such a fright at the unexpected intrusion. The next thing she knew the knob of a boss pushed her off and then began explaining to what was now clearly his wife that it was not what it all appeared to be, some salesman huh?

Kirsty said she then started to piss herself laughing. That was not a good idea. The cuckolded wife was in such a rage that she punched Kirsty right on the face and she busts her mouth wide open. Kirsty of course wanted to punch the wife in return but in the circumstances she knew she was in the wrong. Quickly she gathered her clothes and dashed out of the office. Shona's flatmate joked that one day she would go back and find her knickers. No sweat, stuff happens but what Kirsty had not banked on was that the market had taken a huge slump and even in normally buoyant London the economy was not doing too well at the time. Beggars could not be choosers. Cuts had to be made and there was talk of everyone losing the London allowance. This financial bonus was paid to compensate the high costs of rent and general living expenses in the capital. To make ends meet Kirsty had no other option but to return to work. The buxom blonde responded to an advertisement in the South London Press. 'Telephonist's required - Elephant and Castle £10 per hour.' There was a realistically achievable target bonus to which a monthly bonus could be added. Kirsty called the number displayed on the advertisement. She had little choice as she was by then broke. I got the story through Shona.

Looking very much the streetwise city of London girl, Kirsty went to the interview; looking ultra-smart in her head-turning pin striped business suit. The cleavage was cut a little lower than your average city suit but she thought it necessary to heighten her already considerable appeal. 'Let these puppies out for a walk,' was her comment. Shona's friend was initially shocked when she walked into the interview area and found herself in the company of about twenty other young women. So many girls had responded to the advert and this to her was clear indication of just how bad things had got in the nation's capital. One by one the job applicants were escorted not into an office as they expected but into a downstairs storage area.

The vast basement room was full of large computer-like cabinets and here were flashing LEDs and other lights everywhere to be seen. She said it was like something out of television's Star Trek. Kirsty recalled that she was neither overwhelmed nor under whelmed and had no idea why she was being taken to such a place. She wasn't in the dark for long. The tour was to let her know that all conversations were constantly monitored and recorded. It would have been so much wiser for Kirsty had she known, even at this point, what the job entailed. All was about to be revealed. In a word she was going to learn how to be a telephone whore and she was told that she would thoroughly enjoy the experience and by a happy coincidence it also happened to pay well.

Her initial training was drawn from a massive white board situated at the top of the room. There she was sat with an experienced phone operator. There were many different topics displayed on the high profile white board. The subjects covered anything and everything from holidays to new cars, perhaps twenty topics in all. Underlying all of that the underlying theme that conversational chats were to be sex-based. The mentor who was working the phone when in between calls told her that she should avoid being over explicit. She added that in common with standard practice, and for their own protection she would use a false name. Kirsty was to morph into a cute thing under the name of Chantelle. This personality change was that of an uninhibited freedom loving girl whose language would cause any self-respecting mother to blush.

Several white boards where strategically placed around the large room and some were under the heading of party areas. Here, on a whim, the telephone temptresses would be asked to join in and pretend they were calling like ordinary punters. Of course it was a telephone-based scam and the room was divided into very small cubicles. These were dirty nicotine stained boxes. The filthy burnt red carpets underfoot might have seen better days. The white boards where filled with written inducements, reminders of bonuses and suggestions on how to keep the clients on the telephone thereby bumping up their bill charges. The longer you keep punters on the line the bigger the telephone girl's bonus. Clearly there was money to be made and the bonuses would roll in if she was to see the lighter side of the job. It required a fertile imagination but Kirsty had that in abundance.

She was immediately hooked and took to her new job like a duck takes to water. As brazen as you might expect she had no problem in listening to her client on the other end of the line what they wanted to hear. Our friend would have us in tears of mirth some days as she told us of her conversations with weird callers or saddos as she called them. She had one caller in particular who had a fetish about feet and they spent goodness knows how long talking about feet, shoes, the sensations of sliding one's foot in and out of a lady's shoes. Kirsty said that after she had settled into the job she was beginning to feel less disgust with her clients and was beginning to empathise with them. Imagine, all the lonely people in London who lived for a friendly ear and girls like Chantelle were happy to indulge them. There were some callers who were so sexually depraved that even the normally liberal-minded call centre monitors would disconnect them. However, that didn't happen too often.

One guy was heavily into skat (shitting) and would

describe his fantasy to Chantelle. He asked if her if they could meet up and he could shit in her mouth, smear her body with his crap, shoot his load over her and for the finale he would clean her up with a golden shower. In other disgusting words he would pee all over her. Chantelle declined the suggestion. She would on a daily basis give an update of her conversations and the girls never tired of listening to them.

All in all the girls liked their new living arrangements. Shona called me one day and was absolutely raging with Kirsty after the two had a tiff. That was inevitable I thought to myself as she went on to elaborate and tell me why she was pissed off. Shona had returned home from work earlier than her usual time. She had a migraine and she just wanted to lie down and enjoy a little peace and quiet. I could buy that. Going into her room my sister's unexpected homecoming was revelatory to say the least. She found her friend frolicking stark naked on her bed with a bloke Shona had never before set eyes on.

Shona was outraged at seeing her bed being so defiled. 'What the fuck?' she howled before dragging Kirsty by the hair off the bloke and then off her bed. Shona then began screaming at the bloke 'get the fuck up!' whilst the twat had the cheek to just lay there with an amused grin on his vapid face. He probably mistakenly thought there was going to be a wild cat fight. He was up for enjoying the free unexpected performance. Shona then started chucking bed covers everywhere and she told me she was swearing like a sweetie wife. Kirsty and her so-called friend soon fast exited.

Later, when Shona had calmed down, she spoke with Kirsty. Her wayward friend explained to her that they had been on a bender the entire afternoon. The two had later collapsed on her bed but when they woke she discovered that the slime ball had urinated and wet her divan. As she was still tanked up and thought I was at work she would just use Shona's bed for a little compensation. It was the first of many rows the two would have before Shona would feel obliged to move out. Shona insisted that Sean put a lock on her door after that.

From these and other stories it was clear that Kirsty was something of an oddball and definitely had issues. My sister called a week later. She had a Kirsty update that she wanted to tell me about. This time Shona was laughing hysterically. She said that on this occasion too she had come home early and on arriving home she was desperate for a pee. Immediately flying into the bathroom she dropped her underwear and sat on the toilet seat. As she was splashing she could hear similar water sounds coming from nearby. Then, out of the unexpected blue from behind the shower curtain her friend Kirsty popped her head out and said hello. As she did so Shona said she just sat there with her mouth open, quickly wiped herself and was out of the door as fast as she had come in. Kirsty would later tell her that there was a water shortage and she was doing her bit. Good on you Kirsty!

Shona had not been happy with her temping job at BT and felt that it was time for a change. Shona's life then took an unexpected turn of events. She began working more and more shifts at the bar and decided to give temping a wide berth for a bit. My sister enjoyed the bar work and the socialising that went with it and there were no shortage of romantic offers from the punters as any barmaids will tell you.

When I got lucky enough to catch Shona at home and able to talk she seemed quite distant. I could tell without question that something was worrying her. However, I knew Shona was a tough cookie and more than capable of sorting out her affairs. In retrospect had I been pushier and more persistent I might have saved her from being humiliated. One night in walked a tall blonde lady who, with her short hair, could have been the double of Brigitte Nelson, Sylvester Stallone's wife. The woman was easily 6 foot tall and reasonably well built.

On the night of Shona's mortification she stormed up to the bar and her face was twisted in anger. She pointedly asked to see Shona. My sweet sister was on her break and getting to her feet she told the visitor that she was the woman she was looking for. Was there a problem? There was a problem and the problem was Shona. Next thing my sister knows she is showered with the contents of a large beer. This was followed by a good slapping of her face and she then heard the reason why. 'Keep away from my fucking husband you home fucking wrecker.'

As the woman strode out everyone in the pub stared in astonishment. Then, one by one they came up to the much distressed Shona, sympathised and asked her what that was all about. Ridiculously, Shona had no idea and immediately thought it was a case of a mistaken identity. She didn't even know who the fuck the woman's husband was. Sean then told Shona to go into the back office for a bit of privacy. He told her that he wanted a little chat. As she followed her boss through Shona thought she was getting the tin tack. Whatever, deep down she knew that nothing that was happening was making much sense.

Having invited her to take a seat and taking one himself he says, 'Shona, there is no easy way to tell you this. I only found out for sure myself yesterday. I wanted to find the right time to tell you but I guess that would be now. Terry is married. He has two daughters and he is living with his wife.' Shona's thoughts were best left unsaid and keeping them to herself she left the bar with her head held not quite as high as when she had earlier entered it. Walking home she was in tears. 'The bastard', she thought to herself. He has been playing me like an Irish fiddle. How could that lowlife or any of his gutter friends fail to mention that he was married with kids? Fucking dossers, the whole lot of them thought Shona through a veil of tears. She was not quite sure if she was upset that he was married or because she had been made a laughing stock at her very public humiliation. Shona had no sooner got her key in the door when the telephone rang. She later told me she would not have bothered answering it but she had thought it was me calling her. It wasn't but it was Terry. His conversation began with a plea to her not to put the phone down on him. He then went on to say that he was going to tell her soon. As in his eyes his marriage was finished he had intended leaving his wife to live with Shona.

'Fuck off' says Shona as she places the phone back in its cradle. She then lifted it again to call me. All I could do was give her a shoulder to cry on and to tell her to be very careful. There was something very peculiar about Terry and I thought so from the moment I met him. He was a control freak, a very clingy type and for certain was inclined to stalking. We had both joked that we didn't want Shona rolled up in a carpet and recovered from the bottom of the Thames. There seemed to be a lot of relationships ending on the theme of if I can't have you then no one will.

I kept my concerns to myself but was worried about

my sister. I decided that maybe I should visit her. My studies didn't allow me to take time off so I did what anyone would do in my situation: I threw a sickie as I felt my sister was more important that was what I was doing. As we talked Shona became more upbeat about the turn of events; acceptance and closure can be a wonderful thing. She told me there were no signs that Terry had ever worn a wedding ring. On her guard she had kept her ears and eyes open for any clues as to whether or not he had another life. The bastard had never mentioned that he had kids.

Before I had the chance to book my ticket Shona called again to tell me that she had left the bar. She had found herself a new position working in a car rental place. Sounding excited she saw it as something different and was looking forward to new challenges. Sean had got her the new job. They had become quite good friends and he had told her come back anytime.

Shona started work at the car rental company but complained that the wages were crap for the hours she put in. She added that the owners were Jewish and insisted on paying her cash in hand. Not good as she had to buy her own National Insurance stamps or have a gap in her pension contributions. Shona's excitement at finding her new job was short lived. The owner Amran told her that business was too slow to occupy her but he told her he could get her work answering calls at a cab office where he was the landlord. Fair enough, she decided that it was a good time for a change. This is how she then found herself outside a dilapidated cab office in Wandsworth Road.

As she climbed out of Amram's car her first thought was, you must be shitting me. The place was an absolute dive. The den of iniquity was beyond grotty. The outside of the building looked like it had been last painted a century ago. The windows were filthy and the net curtains she thought at first were black but were in truth screaming out for a good wash. Shona told me that when she walked through the door it had such narrow access it was like being in a little cage. In front of her was a wall. The entrance door to the office, if you could call it that, was to the left of her. Immediately to the right there was a small window area fenced off with chicken wire. The room in which people asked or waited for a cab was the size of an apartment lift.

When Shona and Amran arrived at the cab office the two were greeted by Manny who appeared to emerge from another door. Manny at first sight was a bit of a scary fucker. He was one of the blackest people Shona had ever set eyes upon and given that she lived in London that was saying something. Shona said that Manny gave her one of the friendliest widest smiles that she had ever seen. It was spoiled because he had only two front teeth and they were in the bottom of his cavernous mouth. I remember laughing when Shona was describing him to me. She was telling me that he had upturned fangs at either side and there were no teeth in the middle.

Her new boss sounded an interesting character and as it turned out he was. The fact that Shona found herself in this particular set of circumstances I thought hilarious. I soon discovered that our Shona would happen upon some interesting characters that she would remember for a very long time. She said she was quite taken aback when Manny just seemed to lunge at her and greet her with a bear hug. While Manny chewed the fat outside with Amram, Shona had chance to absorb the surrounding. She couldn't help but notice that the shop front and sidewalk were as disgusting as the place was on the inside. Inside again there was a threadbare carpet and she wondered why they bothered to leave it on the floor. This floor covering was a dark reddish colour she guessed but the stains and cigarette burns where highly visible. The walls had at one time earlier been painted yellow but looked like the inside of an old bar where everyone had smoked heavily over decades. There were several tatty mismatched chairs scattered here and there for drivers to use when waiting for fares. Otherwise there was an old television in the corner of the room and at the moment horse racing was being programmed. A chair and makeshift desk could be seen under old newspapers. The two telephones might have aroused interest at television's Antique Road Show.

Despite all this Shona decided that she would give it a go. She had bills to pay and a job was a job. Amram returned from the other room with Manny and my sister could tell there was an atmosphere between the two men. Peering through the window she could see that there was some kind of heated discussion going on between the two. Manny was waving his arms in the air as if he was ranting and Amram was patiently nodding as he did so. Shona was soon to realise that Manny was a little shy on paying his rent when it was due. Worse, she would be called upon to tell lies on several occasions, telling Amran she didn't know where Manny was. When Amram left the premises Manny offered his latest employee a coffee and showed her into the back room. Talk about basic! To the left was a large double bed and the covers looked rank. Shona said the stench in that room made her gag. There was a large sink which surprisingly was clean and but not the stack of cracked cups and mugs in it. It took Shona a second or two to twig that this was Manny's home.

My sister accepted the offered coffee and the pair then went to the waiting area and took a seat. Manny was very proud of his African roots and Shona soon learned that her new boss despised Jamaicans. In fact, Manny didn't like a lot of races and described most of them as being stupid. He also thought of Amram as being a greedy Jew who was lacking business skills. As Shona and Manny chatted several drivers drifted in, which made my sister feel uncomfortable.

The first driver Shona would meet was a guy named Wassad, of Moroccan nationality; he came through the door shouting like a madman about the fucking Nigerian drivers trying to steal his fare earlier from outside the taxi office. This she was to learn was a common occurrence between cab drivers. Tony, a mixed race guy was the next driver that came through the door. He was quite a tall good looking guy but Tony really had a chip on his shoulder. Apparently he did not like white people. Tony curtly nodded to acknowledge Shona and she in turn welcomed him but she was fixated by what he had in his hand. Having returned from a fare he was drinking Tenant's super lager as if it was perfectly normal for him to do so.

As the drivers trickled in to the office to cover their shifts Shona realised that there were about ten drivers self-employed at the firm. It was only when most of the drivers were present that it dawned on Shona she was the only white face there. The office was situated immediately across from a notorious black housing estate. No wonder she felt like a fish out of water. Shona would soon have an insight into black culture first hand. One good thing about the cab office was that Manny, although he didn't smoke weed himself, had no problem with his drivers smoking it. This was habitual, especially at the weekend. The beer and drugs in the waiting area was full on to say the least.

Despite all this Shona enjoyed working in the cab office. She told me she spent the day doing crosswords. Tony was a bit of a wind up merchant who constantly argued and was always winding the other drivers up, especially the two Nigerian brothers. These two were not very popular with the drivers as they were notorious for loitering outside and stealing fares. Apart from that failing they were respectful guys and mostly kept themselves to themselves.

My sister was beginning to know the regular customers and there was a guy I often heard Shona talk about. A Jamaican called Junior he loved dressing in his national colours. A Rasta man he was popular with the others. He was by the way the local dealer but only in weed and Junior was otherwise very anti hard drugs. Manny on a Friday used to pay Shona 100 bucks and buy her an eighth of weed from Junior. Shona was quite happy with the arrangement. The only problem was that Shona was struggling to find her rent. Besides, she had grown tired of the girls' company so she was soon putting out the feelers that she was looking for a new flat share. Teddy her cousin had in the meantime called Shona to make arrangements for them to go for a beer, which Shona was keen to do. She took the opportunity to tell him that she needed newer cheaper digs. He told her that he knew of somewhere in Peckham.

Teddy gave Shona the address and the two of them arranged to meet up to view the place. My sis' knew the street because it was just round the corner from Teddy. It was a quiet street and that she thought was a big plus.

When they did meet up and reached the new digs Teddy introduced her to her new flat mate. It was not a good start for the young woman looked absolutely wasted. Shona is small built but she looked like a giant when compared with this dwarf-sized waif. Her eyes looked black and skeletal hollow and her name was Alice. She was skeletal and her skin had a sort of yellowy jaundiced type look about it. Shona questioned why Teddy was bringing her to a junky's digs. As though he was reading Shona's mind he explained that he had known Alice for awhile. She was a mate of one of his friends but that was nothing as he pretty much knew everyone in Peckham anyway. In fact Alice was not a junkie although she smoked dope incessantly. Her appearance was mostly due to her being in remission from cancer.

That put things into a different perspective. No way would Shona want to live with a low life junkie. The Big C is a different and unavoidable issue. The two agreed that they would share the rent. Luckily for Shona it was council property. Again Shona wasted no time in saying adios to her old flat mates. From there on she began to spend quite a lot of time with Alice. It must be said that she was yet to see her new friend sober or without a spliff in her lips. Still employed at the cab firm she was in a way envious that Alice could just lie around all day until she reminded herself of why she was unemployed.

My sister one day asked Alice how on earth she could afford to smoke that amount of dope night and day. Her answer was that she could not personally afford to but her mother could help her. She added that her mother thought it therapeutic for her.

I had originally planned to visit my sister after the embarrassment of the pub attack. I had put the idea on hold as at the time money was a problem for me. When I did so my sister met me at Victoria Railway Station. Wasting no time in hitting the nearest bar we sisters caught up as we got a pleasant glow on. From there we afterwards caught a cab to Peckham and this was to be my first meeting with Alice.

I had learned much about my sister's flatmate already as we often discussed her and her health issues. I was a little shocked when I was introduced for she looked worse than I had imagined. During the week I kept my sister's company I accompanied Shona to the cab office where she worked. Yes, her descriptions of the place and the cab drivers were spot on. They were not complimentary.

Whilst Shona was working there she cleaned the place daily including the windows and the curtains. She even took home the cushion covers and washed them. Whatever, despite her best efforts the place was still a flea pit. I thought so anyway but she liked working there, she was comfortable with it and it was hard not to see the reason why. The drivers I felt I already knew from our phone conversations. All the drivers greeted me in a friendly way and I could see that they were genuinely fond of Shona.

Alas such harmony was to be very short lived. Very soon, I would be witnessing a stabbing and believe it or not with a chicken bone. Sitting and chatting contentedly, the pair of us were suddenly distracted by distinct Moroccan shouts on the drive outside the office. Clearly there was an argument going on. Well, there was more than a heated debate for the outraged Moroccan was screaming all kinds of presumed obscenities at the Nigerian. The latter; quite unperturbed by the hysteria allowed the angry North African to vent. It got worse, the Nigerian's condescending grin unsurprisingly further infuriated the Moroccan. The deranged Wassad was now thrusting a chicken bone in the direction of Ebiti. Then from what seemed like out of nowhere he pulled a knife and began stabbing at the now not so happy Nigerian driver. Quickly the other drivers piled out of the cab company's office and dragged the still ranting Wassad away from what was now the scene of a dastardly crime. They hadn't separated the pair quickly enough. The cops had been called and they were on the scene soon enough, sirens screaming everywhere. Poor Wassad, after he had been disarmed he was pushed roughly into the Black Maria police wagon. Ebiti who was far from being as cheerful as he had earlier been was transferred to the ambulance and carted off to Lambeth Hospital. He was not looking too good at all.

That was an unexpected and unwanted very bloody drama. After enquiring as to the cause of the fracas Shona discovered that it was all over a bloody chicken bone. Wassad had been collecting them for his dog. As he bagged them Ebiti was teasing him that they were in fact for his dinner and the rest as they say is history.

Manny drove the pair of us back to Peckham where another type of drama would as quickly unfold. As we entered the flat we could hear really loud dance music. It sounded like one hell of a party was going on and we thought rock and roll party time. Upon our entering the sitting room we realised that it was Alice's own personal party. The girl was bouncing up and down on a makeshift bell-end and, because of the din she was making was unaware of our presence. Shona and I just stood gob smacked at the weird sight of her behaviour. We decided this was neither the time nor the place for us to get a little peace and quiet so we decided that a visit to Teddy was well overdue.

Teddy, being our favourite English cousin, would be pleased to see us even if our visit was unannounced. On our way there we stopped off at the off-licence and dutifully bought some beers as was convention. On arriving there we knew right away that Teddy was at home. He always played the loudest music in the street and we could hear Soul II Soul's - 'Keep on Moving.'

After gaining entry we found that Teddy was absolutely wasted and you could see he had been on a bit of a heavy session. Shona had been a regular visitor but I had not seen him for a while. To me his appearance seemed more ghostlike, if that was possible. Talk about a white shade of pale.

His eyes were completely fucked up but he was as always in very good spirits and we found him too dancing around the room. Teddy that day had company and he introduced us to his mate. Shona had not met him before. She thought the guy looked a bit dodgy but I thought he looked nice enough. He was as wasted as Teddy was and I felt the only solution was for us to play catch-up. Normally I didn't really get into the coke scene but fuck it, I was on holiday. Okay, London is not exactly a 5-star Caribbean location but at the time it was the furthest I had ever travelled from my hometown of Glasgow and I loved it. We four partied all night long and Shona would regret it when she got up for work in the morning. It seemed to be not so long after we crashed in our beds that Shona woke us up. She told us she had to get home, she showered and she then went to work. I was under no illusions. It was going to be the longest of days.

As arranged, Manny picked us up and he was making it obvious that his usual affability was somewhere far behind in a diary somewhere. The cab company boss was not in the best of moods. We were soon to find out just why he was so pissed off. He reckoned that the drivers were messing him around with their settle, this is the money they paid him for using his company's services. 'Those fuckers', as he affectionately called them were leaving him short. This meant he couldn't pay Amram his rent and the landlord was not taking go away for an answer.

Shona none too politely reminded Manny that he was talking shit, for he had been borrowing money from the drivers and in fact he owed them money. They were simply retrieving the loans by deducting it from their settles. Shona had already explained to me that when she first began working in the cab office Manny was completely tee-total and single. But lately he had a new lady in his life or at least claimed as much but we had never met her. He was definitely up to something because he was now to be found only rarely at the cab office. When he did condescend to show himself he was completely bladdered - despite having driven himself back from wherever he had been that day. A good friend of Manny's from way back home, Kofi, had warned him that this woman was no good for him. Manny had deaf ears on that sensitive subject and he refused to listen to reason.

Manny by all accounts was now spiralling into self destruct mode. He was no longer the smart guy in his suits, cutting quite a figure in the shabby locality. He now only occasionally bothered to shave and his appearance had become scruffy. 'Well, he is a grown man and in charge of his own destiny' was Shona's take on things, she wasn't paid to mother him. I was too busy thinking that if he didn't sort himself out soon poor Shona would soon be on the unemployed register again. Shona herself seemed untroubled by the changing circumstances so why should I bother my head about something that had little or nothing to do with me?

Manny was less and less at the cab office and this was also because he was hiding from Amram. It had reached the stage where the landlord was at the end of his tether. He was unprepared to allow the free use of the office for much longer. He had already threatened Manny with eviction for late payment of rent but they always seemed to work things out. The place was a dump and Amram knew it. He probably knew too that if it was vacant it would likely stay that way.

That day was a long day for Shona and me after the previous night carousing with Teddy and his mate. We sisters knew that we needed an early one that night but that was not about to happen. Whenever Manny did his disappearing trick one of the other drivers would give Shona a lift home and Manny would pay for it. On this occasion one of the new drivers, Deon gave us a lift back to Peckham. Deon, the first real Jamaican that I had ever met, was a genuine Jamaican, with the accent to match. I am surprised he hadn't brought a steel band with him. Our new friend had just arrived in England from Jamaica, Kingstown in fact. He was very light skinned and didn't have the usual Jamaican crinkled hair. Something of a short-arse he wasn't too much bigger than Shona and me. My sister had never before met him because her shift ended at 6pm though often it was later than that when she left if she had to wait for an obliging driver. Deon told her that day that he had been working the night shift until now and so the mystery as to why they had never before met was solved. Deon considered himself to be something of an entrepreneur. Not quite unless it was a business called Crack Dealing Unlimited. Crack is definitely bad shit and we wouldn't touch it with a barge pole.

Shona knew that when she told Manny about it if she could catch him sober Manny would deck the so-called entrepreneur. In fact Shona wasted no time in telling her boss and that was the end of Deon. My way or highway was the order of the day.

The week during which I visited my sister flew by. A shame, it had been for me an interesting experience. The evenings we spent together were spent drinking wine, smoking spliffs, chatting and in general just enjoying ourselves whomever's company we were keeping. For me it was nice that I wasn't for once on the end of a phone when keeping up to date with my sister

The week ended all too quickly and before I knew it I was at Victoria Bus Station and on my way back to Glasgow. I loved my home city but I also had a good feeling about London and could see why Shona liked living there. To me she had quite an interesting life and for a short time I felt a little bit envious of her. However, I knew deep down that I would never leave Glasgow. From there on Shona would telephone often and keep me up to date with all the comings and goings and the carrying on's at the cab office. At least I could identify with her working environment and of course her circle of friends and colleagues better. Thankfully there was no more stabbings.

Shona phoned one night and was clearly drunk. I was shocked to hear that Terry had got himself a job in the cab office as a Night Controller. I couldn't believe it. There of all places and London is such a big city so why would Manny give him of all people a job? As it turned out it was not Manny who gave him the job but Amram. Terry was delegated to take the settles from the drivers and so it was obvious that the landlord no longer trusted Manny to do what he was supposed to do, manage the office. When he informed the errant Manny the latter wasn't too fazed but this was likely on account of his being too wasted.

Shona knew from Tony that they had hired a white fucker for the night shift and his name was Terry. It seemed too much of a coincidence so when she learnt this information from Tony she waited until he started his shift to see for herself. She could hardly believe eyes. 'What was a fucking knob head like him doing in a job like that?' she thought to herself. Shona said she never even spoke to him; she drew from him one of her hateful looks and left the office.

I knew instinctively that this situation was not going to have a good outcome and I hate to say it but I was right. About one month after Terry had started she already knew from the other drivers that they did not like him. The fact that he was Caucasian, and a bloke, was enough for them. Shona had confided in Tony about their situation and that Terry was a lying cheating arsehole. Tony agreed and told Shona that long before Terry had started the job he had seen him hanging around the cab office. He had thought it a bit strange and on one occasion Tony had asked him if he was waiting for someone or a cab. Terry had fudged the reply. The fucker in fact was stalking Shona and it went completely unnoticed this was getting creepy. I told Shona that I felt uneasy for her. My sister was not too concerned that Terry might have been a cheating bastard but unlike his brother he was never violent.

I had at this stage been calling Shona on pretty much a daily basis. It was my way of making sure everything was okay for I was concerned for her. On the third day I called I had not heard from Shona and so I phoned the cab office, it was Manny who answered the phone. I asked him if I could speak with my sister. He told me that she had not been into work and nor had she answered the door when someone called around for her. Manny was pretty pissed off that she had blanked work as he had to be the stand-in. I knew that such a thing was out of character for my sister and instinctively thought something must be wrong. Without a pause I replaced the phone and then called Teddy to see if maybe he knew something. Shona and Teddy often went on benders. If anybody knew something, our cousin would be the one to know, that was for certain. The phone kept on ringing and eventually Teddy answered the phone. He apologised but he had not heard it ringing for the music blasting.

Teddy did not know where Shona was either. I got some consolation from his promise that he would call round to the house to see if there was a problem. True to his word Teddy dutifully toddled round to Shona's and began banging on the door. Surely Alice would be in and on hearing the commotion would answer, but the door stayed closed in his face. Teddy did not have a good feeling about all this and decided to do a bit of breaking and entering. Going around to the rear garden he there discovered a broken window. Teddy would later tell me that his adrenaline was sky high when on traipsing around the rear of the building he found the back door open and he used it to gain entry. He explained to me that he found the house deadly silent and that throughout the venture he was on his full guard. As soon as he entered the house he called out Shona and Alice's name; ominously and eerily there was no reply.

He found the place inside was a riot of smashed furniture. The glass table was completely shattered and as he looked around he became more and more ill at ease. By the time he was heading for the kitchen he had availed himself of a large kitchen knife as he was not up for taking chances. He was soon to find out that such preparation was hardly necessary. What was needed was an ambulance for he soon found Shona covered from head to foot in blood. None of us truly know how we would react to suddenly coming across carnage. Teddy would later tell me that he was extremely calm. He had imagined that he would have panicked but no, he had stayed calm throughout the horrid experience.

Immediately, he grabbed the telephone and called the emergency services. Within minutes the ambulance arrived and my sister was blue light taken to Herne Hill Hospital. The police were soon at the apartment too and they were swarming all over the place. Despite his good and brave deed that awful day Teddy told me that the police were hostile towards him. Well, he did have form as he had been in a spot of bother on a few occasions as a kid. Who hasn't? He did know one of the cops.

Teddy explained the situation to them and told them that Shona was his cousin. He then explained about my call and of how he came to be in the house. All was above board. Obviously there was no trace of blood and nothing about his appearance or manner that suggested other than his complete innocence. By that time too he had discarded the kitchen knife he had been prepared to use to defend himself - if he was attacked.

Throughout their questioning the police were completely in the dark as to what might have happened. Teddy also explained that Shona's flatmate, Alice was also missing, this was unusual as she was normally at home. Teddy told me that he could see their enquiring brains ticking over but they were completely clueless. My cousin was then informed that he should swing by the police station and that he would be required to make a statement.

Just as Teddy was leaving Shona's home he told the cops that she was being stalked by an ex boyfriend. Maybe it was important, maybe not. However, in his heart he doubted that Terry would have anything to do with hurting Shona. Of course he was something of a control freak and was interested in her everyday activities but he loved her and so couldn't possibly hurt her. He was so wrong!

I felt so helpless and so very sad for my dear sister. She must have been lying helpless and covered in blood for three days and on her own. I have to admit I wept tears for my sister; she did not deserve that shit. It was then that I made the decision not to tell my mother about what had happened. I would not do so until I knew the full story and that Shona was again safe. I did take it upon myself to call the hospital. The only information they would give me was that she was critical and she was in a bad way. I almost laughed when she finished telling me that she was comfortable. 'Fucking comfortable?' being she was unconscious but in a critical situation. Where do we get them from?

Teddy and Tanya went to Herne Hill hospital to see Shona and to find out what had happened. It was futile for she was heavily sedated and was sleeping throughout our visit. Teddy told me that Tanya had cried when she saw

Shona. Her face had been so badly beaten that her former flatmate could hardly recognise her. Her friend held Shona's hand and prayed as she sobbed her unhappiness.

Teddy told me that the nurse informed him that Shona suffered five stab wounds. She had also suffered broken ribs, her nose was broken and Teddy said you could see from her neck the fading hand prints. Shona suffered lacerations to her hands where she had been frantically trying to defend herself from her attacker. I knew for sure that Shona would have fought like a gladiator. One thing I also knew; whoever did this to Shona would have scratch marks as her nails were like talons. I knew for sure, as we had as kids been on the receiving end of them.

I felt the right thing to do was to call Manny and let him know why Shona had not been at work. No, she was not on a fucking bender. I could hear that Manny was shocked and I also knew that whilst Shona had been working there at the cab firm they had a genuine fondness for each other. Manny was in perfect harmony with everyone in expressing his shock that Shona could have been through such a terrible experience. Everyone was horrified. Shona had such a sweet disposition. Who on earth could have possibly caused her harm?

Whilst speaking with Teddy I told him that Maddie and I would get the train down as soon as we could get ourselves organised. Teddy was quite insistent that there was no need for us to do so as Shona had no shortage of visitors. He would take personal responsibility for looking after his cousin. It was decided that Teddy would call me on a daily basis but I continued to call the hospital as well.

Teddy had taken it upon himself to call into the cab office and he had been there on several occasions to see

Shona. With hindsight I think he had his Sherlock Holmes deerstalker hat on. He was trying to find out if any of the drivers could think of anyone that might harm Shona. He also knew that all of the drivers knew where Shona lived because they had on occasion driven Shona to her home after her shift had finished. Teddy explained to me that he was not quite sure why he went there but he said he was feeling helpless. I knew for sure that if Teddy had found out who had did this to Shona he had better hope that the cops got to him before he did. Our cousin had taken the attack personally as Shona was family, and family is after all is said and done, is still family. Tony was there as usual with a can of Super gripped in his hands.

He told me the atmosphere there was quite sombre; presumably everyone was dispirited because of the attack on Shona. Tony, who normally liked to offensively blank white people mentioned to Teddy that he suspected Terry. Of course Terry was going to be a person of interest to the cops but apparently they now had had trouble locating him. He had mysteriously gone AWOL. Tony told Teddy that he collected his wages from Manny the night before and that Tony had a little friendly word in his shell like ear. Tony had threatened him and told him he would get it if they found out that he was involved. Terry said he would never hurt Shona and Tony let go of his throat.

All we could really do now was wait and see when Shona would wake and then we would know the truth. We assumed that my sister would know who had attacked her. Teddy went to the hospital and when he arrived at Shona's bedside was quite surprised to find his cousin propped up on a pillow and reasonably awake. She also had visitors in the form of the police officers who were questioning her. Teddy said he waited for the cops to leave and was elated to see Shona looking surprising well. He could see beneath the surface however and it was clear she was in much pain but time is the greatest healer of all.

Teddy on seeing her was desperate to ask her who was the bastard that did this to you but before he could open his mouth, she simply said, 'Terry.' Teddy told me he was seething at having his suspicions confirmed and knew that he would have to be dealt with accordingly. Teddy would take care of that.

Shona has always had a fear of hospitals and argued with the doctors that she should be discharged. The medicos were having none of it and persuaded her to wait a couple of days longer. Teddy would soon reveal the mystery of missing Alice. Alice coincidently had taken off for Scotland. She had earlier gone for a week to convalesce in a type of hospice place and was not at home at the time of the attack. We were relieved that Alice was safe. Shona told Teddy she could not possibly return to the flat where she had been attacked. Someone else would have to collect her things, maybe Alice on her return.

This is where Teddy stepped in and offered her a safe haven. Teddy told me that the more he sat there the more agitated he could see Shona was. He had the feeling that Shona would not be spending another night in the hospital. Sure enough, she discharged herself; she signed the disclaimer and then headed back to Teddy's place courtesy of Manny. He had come to the hospital with flowers. Shona said she got a lot of strange looks when he did so. The question on enquiring faces was obvious. Why is this old black dude visiting and giving you flowers. Shona shrugged their inquisitiveness off; in fact it made her smile.

Shona was in a bad way but I was so glad that we

could at least talk again. I knew for sure she was in a lot of pain and up until now she did not understandably want to talk about what happened. A while passed before Shona would initially confide in Teddy. Teddy had been a godsend for Shona. Aunt Bella had insisted that she would look after my sister but Shona preferred to be at Teddy's place. She was at this stage pretty much back to normal but obviously had scars and not all of them of a physical nature. Nevertheless she was on the mend.

Teddy was keen to know the whole story but wisely decided to bide his time. She would tell all; but when she chose to, and not when it was coaxed out of her. When she did reveal what had happened she told Teddy that she had been asleep and alone in the house at the time. She had awoken to the sound of breaking glass. Clearly frightened she summoned up enough courage to rise from her bed and to go and see what was going on. It must have been a formidable challenge for her to do so as she was painfully aware that she was alone in her home.

Moving quietly towards the kitchen from where the sound of breaking glass had came from she suddenly felt herself painfully and roughly dragged back by a fist curled up in her hair. With her attacker being stronger and having the element of surprise the poor girl never had a chance. She felt herself being dragged back into her bedroom and thrown roughly on to her bed. The next thing her attacker was straddling her with his hands clasped around her throat. In the dim light she must have been met with a sight that was more shocking than one's worst nightmare, but this was for real. Shona said Terry looked like a man possessed. There could be no reasoning with him, he was demonic and in a trance like state. Shona was no match for her attacker as over and over again he kept repeating a mantra of hate words, 'it only takes four minutes, it only takes four minutes, it only takes four minutes...'

Shona in her horror and pain realised the significance of his mantra; it only takes four minutes to strangle the life from someone. Shona said she is not sure how she did it but she had such an adrenaline rush that she managed to somehow get him off her. Her victory was to be short-lived for as she struggled for breath and to come to terms with the searing pain in her tortured throat her lovelorn lover calmly walked into the kitchen. When he returned he was armed with one of her carving knives. Shona was of course terrified at the finality of his intentions. It was so out of character. She had never known Terry to be of a violent nature. How wrong could she be? He was clearly intent on taking her life.

As he approached her, the already sinister atmosphere became more terrifying. As she was recovering her breath she held her hands and arms up in an instinctive shield. It was a futile gesture. Her attacker then began to again chant a mantra as though he was fixated by his own words of hate. It was as if his words were fuelling his hatred, as if inner demons were urging him to do as they intended him to do. In the half light shafting from her bedroom window she could see the light shining off the knife's blade as it rose before its intended plunge to hack away at her. Ceasing his mantra he rasped that she had two choices. He could just kill her and be done with it or he could hack her face to pieces so no one would ever again find her attractive.

My sister was desperately trying to reason with him, to bring him back from whatever abyss his insanity had cast him. Terry was in no mood for debate or reasoning. Undeterred, he was on a mission to kill or harm her and he would not be frustrated. Lurching closer to her he raised the knife again. She tried to defend herself of course but with what, bare arms and wailing, protests and screams? The blood spurted and she knew he had done what he intended to do to her. Everything became a blur, even the slashing and the thrusting. She was never aware until afterwards how many times he had thrust the knife into her.

In his insanity he dragged her around the room with one hand, her blood spurting as with his free hand he set about wrecking everything in sight. Having smashed to pieces a chair he dispensed with the knife and picking up one of the broken chair legs he wielded it time after time. Using it as a club he struck her repeatedly as rapidly she fell to the floor and unconsciousness beckoned to ease her from the miseries he was inflicting upon her.

Shona was mournful as she lamented what her feelings had been as death stood ready to claim her. She comforted herself that soon the pain would soon pass and that she would sleep without waking. At least she would be at peace. Such as death even horrifying met would have been a relief but as she drifted in and out of consciousness, her only beacon the savage pain that threatened to consume her, he raped her repeatedly. It was as brutal and as painful as had been the thrusts of the knife he had earlier wielded.

As she recounted her tale Teddy could feel his heart was close to bursting and the tears were threatening to flow. Impulsively he reached out and held Shona close to him. He did so as much to prevent the tears from flowing for his doing so brought relief from the agonies both were going through. Soon the both were weeping copiously as they clung to each other. Somehow it symbolised the triumph of love over the hatred of violent death.

From there on my beautiful sister Shona was determined that she was not to be a victim but to be instead a survivor; she would triumph over evil. Just as clearly she knew she had to turn her back on all that had happened and to move on. It could never again be Peckham. There could be no turning back.

When well enough, Shona returned to the cab office and was taken aback at the warm and affectionate welcome. Even those drivers she had not had a particularly good relationship with, warmly greeted her; some hugging and sympathising with her. Expressing herself in such terms of affection did not come easily to Shona so her return to the cab firm's office must have been something of an ordeal too. It was a door she had to walk through and to then afterwards close behind her.

Shona never told anyone else about her being raped as she was shamed by her additional humiliation. Many years would pass until she confided in me. She knew Teddy would never betray her and he did not, of course. Shona heard that Terry was in intensive care somebody, and nobody put their hands up, had taken it on themselves to find him and to give him a taste of his own medicine.

We had our own thoughts but we kept them to ourselves. Shona is a much more forgiving person than I am but I knew I will always be eternally thankful for whoever got their revenge. The police had their own ideas too and they were at his bedside when Terry came out of his coma. When he emerged from his own darkness he was cautioned and charged with the attempted rape and murder of my sister. Shona finally moved to Brixton and had been living there for about six months when the phone rang. Teddy was at the other end of the call.

'Shona, I have something to tell you.' My sister had no reason to listen further for she knew that she was soon to return to her home city of Glasgow.

www.ingramcontent.com/pod-product-compliance
Ingram Content Group UK Ltd.
Pitfield, Milton Keynes, MK11 3LW, UK
UKHW041946190726
13854UKWH00004B/1827